"Love me now, Jason," Daisy pleaded. "I need you."

His heartbeat accelerated. "I believe you do." He paused. "Here, on the mountain, in the moonlight?"

Her own heart gave a wild leap and she kept her cheek pressed to his chest. "Yes. Right here, right now. Will you do it?"

"If I was a nice guy like my brother, I'd say no." He pushed her away and smiled recklessly down at her. "But I'm no angel and I've always been one to take advantage of the moment. Lord knows we may never have anything else." He pulled his sweater over his head and tossed it on the ground. "I've wanted you too passionately to be choosy about the way I get you." He unbuttoned his shirt and dropped it on top of the sweater. "Take off your gown."

Her aggressiveness vanished, and she felt suddenly shy.

"Shall I do it?" He didn't wait for an answer but began to unfasten the tiny buttons marching down her bodice. "It's strange how a period gown makes a man feel."

"How does it—" She gasped as his hands brushed her skin.

"Like a brigand. Definitely like a man from another age, one who had no rules when he wanted a woman. All those hours I sat in the cottage and watched your father paint you in this dress, I thought about how I'd like to unbutton you like this. I began to have all kinds of fantasies, about how I'd sit there with you in my lap, and you'd let me do anything I wanted to you."

She moaned at the erotic images his words painted, and at the sensation of his hands caressing her bare back.

"Wouldn't you?" he muttered. There was no answer. "Tell me."

"Yes. . . ."

WHAT ARE *LOVESWEPT* ROMANCES?

They are stories of true romance and touching emotion. We believe those two very important ingredients are constants in our highly sensual and very believable stories in the *LOVESWEPT* line. Our goal is to give you, the reader, stories of consistently high quality that may sometimes make you laugh, sometimes make you cry, but are always fresh and creative and contain many delightful surprises within their pages.

Most romance fans read an enormous number of books. Those they truly love, they keep. Others may be traded with friends and soon forgotten. We hope that each *LOVESWEPT* romance will be a treasure—a "keeper." We will always try to publish

LOVE STORIES YOU'LL NEVER FORGET
BY AUTHORS YOU'LL ALWAYS REMEMBER

The Editors

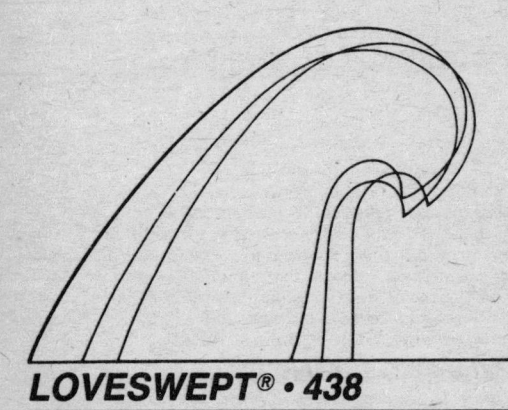

LOVESWEPT® • 438

Iris Johansen
An Unexpected Song

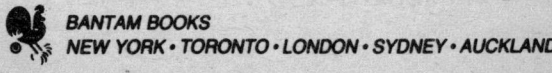

BANTAM BOOKS
NEW YORK • TORONTO • LONDON • SYDNEY • AUCKLAND

AN UNEXPECTED SONG

A Bantam Book / December 1990

LOVESWEPT® and the wave device are registered trademarks of Bantam Books, a division of Bantam Doubleday Dell Publishing Group, Inc. Registered in U.S. Patent and Trademark Office and elsewhere.

If you would be interested in receiving protective vinyl covers for your Loveswept books, please write to this address for information:

Loveswept
Bantam Books
P. O. Box 985
Hicksville, NY 11802

ISBN 0-553-44069-1

Published simultaneously in the United States and Canada

Bantam Books are published by Bantam Books, a division of Bantam Doubleday Dell Publishing Group, Inc. Its trademark, consisting of the words "Bantam Books" and the portrayal of a rooster, is Registered in U.S. Patent and Trademark Office and in other countries. Marca Registrada. Bantam Books, 666 Fifth Avenue, New York, New York 10103.

PRINTED IN THE UNITED STATES OF AMERICA

OPM   0 9 8 7 6 5 4 3 2 1

One

"Your little discovery can't be that good," Jason Hayes said dryly. "If she was, she'd be in New York or London, not Geneva, Switzerland."

"She's terrific." Eric settled back in his seat and glanced around the theater. It was a small house, but every seat was filled. "You can see how she packs them in."

"It's *Les Misérables* that packs them in. The music has magic."

"No, I tell you, it's her," Eric protested. "Would I have insisted on bringing you all the way here from New York if I hadn't thought you'd like her? Her voice is spectacular. If you didn't insist on cast approval, I would have tried to sign her up for Desdemona when I heard her last week. She's the best soprano I've ever—"

"Stop." Jason held up his hand. "I've heard it all before."

Eric looked intently at him. "Lord, you're a cynical bastard. That's your problem. You're spoiled rotten and there's nothing you haven't heard or seen. Where's your joie de vivre?"

Jason grinned. "You've got enough for both of us."

"And I'll keep it alive and well until I'm six feet under." Eric's square, boyish face lit with a mischievous smile. "Life's too much fun for me to be tempted into become a brooding Rochester like you."

Jason smiled crookedly. "The comparison is certainly apt."

"Damn," Eric muttered. "Hey, I'm sorry. You know what a big mouth I have."

"No offense." Jason glanced down at the program. "Her name is Daisy Justine?"

"Yes," Eric said absently, gazing at Jason. "You're looking tired as hell."

"I'll be all right. I can take a rest now. I finished the changes on the score for the last act right before I stepped on the airplane."

"The score didn't need changes."

"A score can always be made better."

"So speaketh the perfectionist. You work too hard. Peg and I haven't seen you for over eight months."

Jason kept his gaze on the program. "You know why."

"Yeah." Eric frowned, troubled. "But it has to stop. You can't go on like this."

"Why not?" Jason turned the page of the program. "You said I was spoiled rotten."

"I was joking." Eric paused. "You have to do something about it."

Jason knew he was no longer talking about getting more rest. "I've tried."

"I know, but there has to be a way to stop it. You can't protect the whole world."

"I don't protect the whole world." Jason smiled. "Just my corner of it."

"I don't like to see you like this. I remember when—"

"There's no use looking back," Jason said quietly. "And I live a good life. I have everything I want. Money, women, success. Stop thinking of me as a tragic figure."

Eric shook his head. "It's not enough."

No, it wasn't enough, and he should have realized that Eric, who knew him best, wouldn't buy his rationalizations. "I have my work."

Eric nodded. "If you didn't, you'd be crazy by now. Your music is the only thing that means a damn thing to you."

"Not entirely. I have a trifling fondness for you."

"Stop kidding. You're the greatest composer the stage has seen in this century, but there's got to be—"

"Andrew Lloyd Webber wouldn't agree with you."

"The audience and the critics do. Stop arguing with me."

Jason smiled. "I have no intention of doing so. My ego won't permit it."

"But you've become an almost complete recluse. You can't live only for your work."

"Who said? Watch me."

Eric sighed. "Dammit, you're stubborn."

Jason smiled affectionately. "You're the one who's hanging on to the subject, my fine bulldog." His smile faded. "Drop it, Eric."

Eric studied his expression and then nodded reluctantly. "Okay." He lowered his voice as the lights dimmed and the orchestra struck up the overture. "If I can't save you from yourself, at least

I can feed your passion by serving Daisy Justine up to you."

Jason chuckled. "You sound like a pimp. I'm not in the market for a new bedmate."

"I wasn't talking about your carnal urges. You go through women like a hay fever victim goes through tissues." Eric grimaced. "That's not your passion, that's only lust."

"And what is my passion, O seer?"

"The songs," Eric said simply. "And the voices who sing them." The curtain was beginning to swing open as he added with satisfaction, "She's going to knock your socks off."

Jason shrugged. "We'll see." He wished he could exhibit more enthusiasm. Hell, Eric was probably right and he was becoming jaded. Maybe the woman was good, but she couldn't be as fantastic as Eric claimed. In spite of Eric's keen business sense that made him a top-notch producer, he was prone to occasional wild lapses in judgment when it came to talent. Well, the least he could do was give her a chance.

He settled back in his seat as the musical began to unfold before his eyes. He had gotten off the plane from New York only three hours earlier and was finding it difficult to stay awake, much less concentrate. As he had said, the music was fantastic, but he had seen the play too many times for it to hold him. For a regional production the set was surprisingly good, the cast, too, but not good enough to merit special attention in this first scene.

"Here she is." Eric grasped his arm as soon as the factory scene started, nodding to a slim, golden-haired woman in a cornflower-blue peasant gown.

She certainly looked the part of Desdemona, Jason thought objectively. Daisy Justine possessed a riveting stage presence and was truly exquisite. A little above average height, she moved with extraordinary grace. She had generously-sized breasts and roses-and-cream complexion. Her long white-gold hair and delicate features gave her an air of angelic luminosity. Yes, that was the term. She shone as if lit from within.

"See?"

"The only thing I see right now, Eric, is that she looks like Desdemona." And that he was having an undeniable physical response as he looked at her, Jason realized with astonishment. He was dead tired, jet-lagged, and never before been attracted to the ethereal type, yet he could feel an unmistakable stirring in his groin as he looked at the woman.

Eric muttered something beneath his breath.

Then the scene switched to Fantine, racked by despair, kneeling alone on the stage to sing her big solo, "I Dreamed a Dream."

Jason stiffened, and he heard Eric's low chuckle.

Clear golden notes filled with beauty and passion soared through the theater. She *lived* the song, let it take her, became one with it.

"My God," Jason whispered. He experienced a fierce joy that was close to pain. He was lost, swept away, and for the remainder of the time she was on the stage, he sat transfixed, riveted, his gaze never leaving the luminous figure of Daisy Justine.

When the lights went up at the end of the first act, Eric turned to him. "Well?"

Jason forced his hands to release their grip on

the arms of the seat and got to his feet. "Let's get the hell out of here."

"Now? Don't you want to wait and go backstage to see—" Eric broke off as he saw Jason striding up the aisle through the crowd. He got hurriedly to his feet and caught up with him as he reached the lobby. "What the hell is wrong with you? Dammit, I know you liked her."

"Yes." Jason's voice was clipped as he pushed through the crowd.

"Then let's go get her. She's not on again until the last scene."

"We'll wait until the show's over. Let's find someplace to have coffee." Jason welcomed the cool air on his face as he started down the street toward the café on the corner. Heaven knew he needed something to clear his head. He felt punch drunk. "What do you know about her?"

"That she sings like an angel and can act to boot."

"What else?"

Eric fell into step with him. "I talked to the director, Hans Keller, and he said she was good-natured, always on time, thoroughly professional. She studied with Stoloni in Milan on a scholar-ship. She's twenty-four, mother dead, and lives with her father in a cottage in an artists' colony on the outskirts of Geneva. He's an artist."

"Any good?"

Eric shrugged. "Mediocre." He glanced at Jason curiously. "What difference does it make? We're hiring the woman, not her father."

Jason avoided the question. "Why is she play-ing in a two-bit production when she should be on Broadway?"

"How do I know?" Eric asked with a touch of

irritation. "Look, do you approve of her as our first choice for Desdemona or don't you?"

"I approve." Jason opened the door of the café and a bell tinkled merrily, announcing their arrival. As a tuxedo-garbed waiter hurried toward them from across the room, Jason muttered, "Do you think I'm an idiot? She's absolutely mesmerizing."

Eric smiled jubilantly as he followed his brother. "Now you're talking. So we sign her tonight?"

Jason gazed blindly at the cozy, damask cloths as he followed the waiter to a table. Eric was right, he was acting weird as hell and he couldn't seem to control it. His reaction to Daisy Justine had been incredibly intense, more intense than Eric could possibly guess.

It was the music, he assured himself. How long had he waited for a voice like that? His response was to the music, not to the woman.

But somehow the woman and the music had melded, become one in his mind.

And that "one" had become completely, over-whelmingly *his.*

He had sat there in the theater, wave after wave of fierce jealousy deluging him as the audience had applauded her. He didn't want to share those moments. He didn't want to share *her.*

He sat down at a table, accepted the menu from the waiter, glanced at it, and then handed it back. *"Café."* He had never been a possessive man, and his response was crazy. But then, every emotion he experienced since first seeing Daisy Justine was crazy. Lord, he was completely irra-tional about her. Eric must be right, he'd been working too hard.

Daisy Justine *was* Desdemona—and a voice

like hers didn't come down the road every day. Once he had recovered his equilibrium, it would give him immense satisfaction to have her sing his lyrics.

Baffled, Eric gazed at him. "You look like you're wrestling with the fate of the world. Just tell me what you want to do."

"Naturally, we'll sign her tonight," Jason said impatiently. "I couldn't accept anyone else for Desdemona now."

Eric breathed a sigh of relief and then suddenly chuckled. "Lord, she really knocked you out, didn't she? I can't wait for your reactions when she sings your songs. I've never seen you like this way before."

At the moment Jason didn't want to envision Daisy Justine singing his songs. His reaction had been too strong, completely out of proportion to the situation. How much stronger would he react if he heard that exquisite voice singing his music?

Nonsense! When he met the woman she would probably be as banal and empty-headed as a wax doll and he would have no trouble separating the woman from the song. An odd pang of apprehension shot through him. For some reason he didn't want to meet Daisy Justine, felt it was dangerous to meet her.

"I'm just tired." He avoided Eric's gaze as the waiter set a steaming cup of coffee in front of him. "I think I'll let you go alone to her dressing room and handle the offer. I'll wait backstage for you."

"I'm sorry, I can't do it." Daisy felt her throat tighten as she said the words. Lord, it was difficult to turn Eric Hayes down when the fact that he had asked her at all seemed a miracle.

Eric looked at her in astonishment. "Isn't the money good enough? We can negotiate."

"The money's fine. I'd do the role for nothing to be in a Jason Hayes musical."

"You've heard of him?"

"This is Switzerland, not Timbuktu. Everyone knows Jason Hayes." That wasn't quite accurate. Certainly everyone knew the man's work, but that was all. He was the quintessential mystery man, publicity shy, reclusive, eccentric. On occasion he had been known to miss his own opening night. Daisy turned back to the mirror and started creaming the makeup from her face. "I have the cast albums from every show he's ever done. His music . . ." She trailed off and swallowed to ease the knot in her throat. "He's wonderful."

"*Night Song* is the best thing he's ever done. It's an adaptation of Shakespeare's *Othello*. It's been a dream of Jason's to do the play since we were boys." Eric's voice lowered coaxingly. "You'd play Desdemona. It's the role of a lifetime."

She wished he'd just be quiet and go away. She didn't want to hear any more. The role she'd play in that marvelous plot was irresistible: The smoldering obsessive jealousy of the warrior moor that doomed the love he shared with his gentle bride. "I can't do it."

"Why not? It would make you."

She forced a smile. "I'd be a pretty weak person if I let a role make or break me. No, it's simply that I can't leave Geneva."

"You'd rather live here than become an international star?"

"I don't care much about fame." She turned to

face him and said gently, "Thank you for making this offer, but I really can't do it. Now, if you'll excuse me, I'd like to get dressed. I'm very tired."

Eric reluctantly rose to his feet. "I wish you'd reconsider. Jason is going to throttle me."

"I won't reconsider. Good luck finding your Desdemona."

Eric shook his head and turned toward the door. "I don't think Jason will—" He broke off and a moment later the door closed behind him.

Daisy turned back to the mirror and stared blindly at her reflection. She had received wonderful offers before, but never one of this magnitude or allure. A Jason Hayes musical was a singer's dream. He wrote music that could touch the heart and send the spirit soaring. Dear heaven, she wanted the role.

Well, she couldn't have it and she had to accept that knowledge with serenity.

Easy words, but they didn't stop the aching frustration surging through her.

A Jason Hayes musical . . .

"She turned us down."

Jason straightened away from the stage door against which he had been leaning as Eric walked toward him. "What?"

"You heard me. She turned the offer down."

"Offer her more money."

"She said it wasn't a question of money. She doesn't want to leave Geneva."

Jason muttered a curse beneath his breath. "It doesn't make sense."

Eric shrugged. "She seems pretty determined."

"Maybe she's just trying to drive up the price."

"I don't think so." Eric frowned. "She's pretty straightforward. I like her, Jason. She seems the same onstage and off. She has a kind of simplicity, but she . . . glows."

"Then we need her for Desdemona."

"I don't believe we're going to get her."

"The hell we're not," Jason said harshly. He felt again that surge of fierce possessiveness he had experienced in the theater. Dammit, he wouldn't let her walk away from him. "There has to be a way." He started down the dimly lit corridor. "Wait for me. I'll be back in a minute."

"You're going to talk to her?"

"No," Jason said grimly. "I'm going to sign her."

"Miss Justine, I'm Jason Hayes."

Daisy unconsciously tensed and stepped back from the door. It appeared Eric Hayes had sent in the big gun. "How do you do, Mr. Hayes? I'm a big fan of yours."

"Evidently not big enough to persuade you to star in my play," he said curtly as he entered the dressing room and shut the door.

Very big gun. Jason Hayes was nothing like his brother in either appearance or character, and Daisy immediately felt threatened. He was as far from the stereotype of a sensitive musician as one could imagine. Not only was he dark while Eric was blond, Jason stood well over six feet and was as powerfully built as a prizefighter. His skin was tanned to a shade close to bronze, and his features were not conventionally good-looking. His cheekbones were too broad, his brows a black slash over piercing blue-green eyes, his well-shaped mouth too sensual. Othello, she thought suddenly, and then smiled in amusement at the whimsy. He was probably nothing like Shakespeare's brooding, possessive warrior. "I meant no insult," she said gently. "I love your music."

"And I love your voice." His sudden smile lit his dark face with warmth, and the air of grimness vanished. "I want it—and I mean to have it."

"I explained to your brother that I can't possibly do—"

"What do you want?" he asked bluntly. "Tell me and I'll give it to you."

She wanted to star in his play and sing his songs but he couldn't give it to her. "It's not possible."

"Why not?"

"Personal reasons."

His gaze narrowed on her face. "A lover?"

She sensed a sudden tension in him that bewildered her. "I'd rather not discuss it."

"You intend to waste an opportunity like this for an affair?" he asked harshly.

"I didn't say—" She broke off and said quietly, "People are more important than careers. Love is more important."

"So saccharine, Ms. Justine. You can't be—" He stopped, studying her face. "I'll be damned. You mean it."

She nodded. "Of course I mean it. I don't say things I don't mean."

"How rare."

A luminous smile lit her face. "Perhaps in New York, not here."

"I'd wager it's just as rare on this side of the Atlantic." He smiled curiously. "I believe I'll have to investigate the phenomenon."

"I wouldn't bother. It would be a waste of your

talent. You'd do better to concentrate on your wonderful music. I'm sorry, but I really can't work with you, Mr. Hayes, and I—"

"Jason."

She ignored the interruption and started to turn away. "As I told your brother, the question isn't open to negot—" She broke off as his hand grasped her wrist.

Electricity. Heat. Vibrant magnetism.

She looked up, startled, and saw an expression of shock on his face that must have reflected her own. She felt curiously breathless and was suddenly conscious of how close he was, the heat his big body was emitting, the scent of soap and lime aftershave lotion.

His hand released its grip on her wrist. "I'm sorry. I didn't mean to touch you." His tone was suddenly fierce. "But you were running away from me, dammit."

She moistened her lower lip with her tongue. "Because I assumed our discussion was over. You made an offer and I refused."

"It's not over. It's only just begun." He took a step back and obviously tried to temper the fierceness in his voice. "Let me take you out to dinner and we'll talk some more."

She shook her head. "It would be futile. I won't change my mind."

He gazed at her a moment, his blue-green eyes fixed intently on her face. Then he smiled again, not mockingly or cynically but warmly. "Then I suppose I'll have to change it for you. I won't give you up."

The phrasing was strangely possessive, and she again experienced a great surge of wariness. "You can't give up what you don't have."

"A slip of the tongue." His eyes twinkled. "Naturally, I meant I won't give up my Desdemona."

"Naturally." She relaxed. Of course that was what he meant. "Now, if you'll excuse me, I want to go home and get to bed. I live outside Geneva, and it's a long drive."

"I'll take you."

"No," she said firmly.

His smile remained in place, but she was conscious of a subtle tensing of his muscles. "I'm not giving up. You were born to sing Desdemona."

She said with forced lightness, "Perhaps someday you'll let me star in one of the touring companies here in Europe."

He shook his head. "I want you to create the role. I want you on Broadway." He turned and opened the door. "Good night, Daisy."

He had used her first name, and for some reason the sudden drop in formality added to her uneasiness. "Good night, Mr. Hayes."

He glanced over his shoulder and again corrected her. "Jason."

Before she could answer he had shut the door behind him.

"So what do we do now?" Eric asked Jason as he got out of the taxi at the Hilton. "We can't force her to come with us."

"No." Jason paid the taxi driver and turned and strode toward the front entrance of the hotel. "But we can find an edge and use it."

"What edge?"

"Whatever it takes." Jason entered the lobby. "But there's no need for both of us to cool our heels here. Take a plane to London tomorrow and see what you can do about signing Colin Bartlin for Iago. I'll handle everything here."

Eric frowned. "You're sure?"

Jason nodded. "It may take a while to get him. I hear Bartlin's got a long-term contract with *Phantom.* Why don't you call Peg and have her meet you there?"

"I may do that." He brightened and fell into step with Jason as they crossed the lobby toward the bank of elevators. "She's never been to London, and she needs a break. The kids have been driving her crazy lately." He pressed the button for the elevator. "If you're certain you don't mind becoming involved in the Justine negotiations."

He was already involved, Jason thought grimly. It wasn't just the music. He had only touched her and his body was still aching and aroused. She had felt the chemistry, too, in spite of her devotion to that damn lover who seemed to hold her in thrall.

He felt a surge of red-hot fury at the thought and drew a steadying breath. It was only sex. It wasn't uncommon for a man to feel an obsessive sexual attraction—and control it. There would be no danger to her. He would sign her. They might have a few nights together to rid themselves of their shared lust, then he would go back to New York.

The doors slid open and he stepped into the elevator. "Don't worry. I have nothing better to do right now. I don't anticipate any problem with eventually persuading Daisy Justine to sign with us."

Though it was well after midnight, her father was still up when Daisy arrived at the cottage.

She hadn't expected him to be asleep, though. Lately he was totally wrapped up in his work. He had gotten into the habit of rising at dawn and continuing to paint until well after midnight.

She shut the door. "Hi, Charlie."

"Hi," he said absently.

She shook her head resignedly as she saw his tall, gawky frame hunched before the easel standing across the large room that was their living and studio space. The strong lights picked up the gray streaks in Charlie's disheveled brown hair and the paint splotches on his favorite blue chambray work shirt. "It's after midnight. Time for bed."

"In a minute. I want to get the hue of this bowl just right. . . ." His gaze narrowed on the canvas. "How did it go tonight?"

"Pretty well. The audience seemed to think I was okay." She strolled over to the canvas and laid her head against his arm as she studied the painting. "I like this one. That banana looks real enough to eat."

He grimaced. "As an art critic once told me, I have a great grasp of texture and no grasp of soul."

"Which just goes to show you what an idiot he was. How can a banana have a soul?"

He chuckled. "That's what I thought at the time. I remember how outraged I was . . ." He trailed off as he became lost in his painting again.

"Did you eat supper?"

"What?" He glanced down at her. "I think so. Chili or something."

"That was yesterday." Her worried gaze ran over him. He had always been slender, and his tall, spare frame was now growing thinner every day, she noticed uneasily. The feverish energy he was injecting into his work was taking its toll.

"Was it?" He added a little gray to the cobalt of the bowl containing the fruit. "Well, I'm sure I had something."

"I'll make some soup for us." She threw her purse on the couch and moved toward the tiny kitchenette across the room. "And then we'll go to bed."

"After I finish." He hesitated. "I thought maybe, if you weren't too tired, you'd pose for a little while for me. The portrait has something—it *feels* good, Daisy."

"Then why won't you let me see it?"

"It's a surprise."

"I'm not tired, but you have to rest. You know what the doctor said about—" She stopped. He had turned to look at her and was smiling gently as he slowly shook his head. They both knew it was only a matter of time, but he had made her promise to tell no one and live each minute to the hilt. She didn't have the right to lecture him about how he should spend his last days simply because she wanted to keep him with her a little longer. She felt the tears rise to her eyes and quickly turned away so he wouldn't see them. "We'll talk about it later. I'll make the soup."

Charlie worked on her portrait until after three in the morning and stopped then only because Daisy firmly sent him off to bed on the pretext that she was too tired to pose any longer. He carefully draped the portrait before he left the room. After the door of his bedroom shut behind him, she got up and returned to the canvas of the still life her father had been working on earlier.

It wasn't really a very good painting. Just a still life like a dozen others that were displayed by hopeful artists in the colony. It wasn't fair, dammit. All Charlie had ever wanted was to create something wonderful. He had worked hard all his life to achieve that goal. Why couldn't the muse have blessed her father with just one work that he could be justifiably proud of before he died?

She wearily turned away and switched off the lights before moving toward her own small bedroom. Life wasn't always fair, but one had to make the best of it. They had these last few months together, and maybe tomorrow Charlie would paint his masterpiece.

She took off the sky-blue eighteenth-century gown in which Charlie had insisted on painting her and carefully hung it in the closet. The first time he had seen her play Fantine he had said that she was born to wear a period costume, and when he had decided to paint her portrait, nothing would do but that she buy this gown from the company.

She put on her nightgown and went to the window and threw it open. There was no use trying to go to sleep until she wound down a little. Too many things had happened tonight, and the adrenaline was still flowing. The Alps looked austere in the moonlight, and she shivered a little as she gazed at them. She much preferred the view in the sunlight, when she could see the lush grass on the foothills. Then she was always reminded of that wonderful scene in *The Sound of Music*. Now all the softness was gone and the mountains seemed only to exude hard, craggy power.

Like Jason Hayes, she thought suddenly. He possessed the same air of bold, irresistible power as the mountains. Yet there was nothing cold about the man. She had been conscious of volcanic heat underlying his rugged exterior.

Night Song.

Her throat tightened painfully and she swallowed with difficulty. She couldn't let herself think about Jason Hayes or his play. She had turned down other offers in these last few years. The pain would go away in time. It was the joy of singing that was important, not her career itself.

But, dear heaven, how she would have loved to be the first one to sing his songs for Desdemona.

Two

At two-thirty the next afternoon there was a knock on the front door of the cottage.

"I'll get it." Daisy stood up from the huge thronelike chair, jumped down from the platform, and quickly moved across the room toward the door. "Keep immortalizing me. I want to look at least as appetizing as your banana. I think I deserve that for—"

She stopped as she threw open the door.

Jason Hayes stood on the doorstep. His gaze wandered over her in the square low-necked blue gown, and he smiled faintly. "You really believe in living a part, don't you? Very nice. May I come in?"

Panic raced through her. "No."

His brows lifted. "I beg your pardon?"

She glanced hastily over her shoulder. Charlie was absorbed in the painting in front of him, but there was no telling when he might glance up. "Go away. I can't talk to you now."

"Is your lover so jealous?" His lips tightened. "I thought you lived with your father."

"I do." She stepped closer and half closed the door to block Charlie's view of Jason Hayes. "Go away," she snapped. "I told you that I—"

"I have no intention of going away." He paused. "Until I get what I want."

"I'm not going to—" She broke off as she saw his determined expression. He wasn't going to give up. "You can't come in. I'll change and meet you at the Zeider Café down the street in an hour."

She shut the door in his face and turned around just as Charlie glanced up inquiringly.

She shrugged casually as she strolled back toward the platform. "Someone collecting for a charity. Nothing important."

Jason Hayes stood outside the café, his expression distinctly revealing how displeased he was as he watched Daisy walk toward him. She could scarcely blame him, she thought ruefully. It had been closer to two hours than one before she had been able to get away without arousing Charlie's suspicion. Half the musical world kowtowed before Jason Hayes, and her rudeness must be disconcerting, to say the least.

"At last," he said caustically. "I was afraid the local gendarmes were going to arrest me for loitering."

"Why didn't you go inside and have a cup of coffee?"

"I didn't want coffee." He took her arm and started down the shop-lined street. "Let's walk. My temper's a little ragged, and I need to work it off."

"You have no right to be angry. I didn't invite

you here." The light touch on her arm was sending the same electrical awareness through her that she had experienced the night before. She casually disengaged herself and edged away from him. "In fact, I thought I'd made my feelings very clear."

"I didn't expect to have the door slammed in my face."

"That was rude." She didn't look at him. "I didn't want my father to know about your offer."

"Why not?"

"It would have made him unhappy. He would have felt he was keeping me from an opportunity."

"And is he?"

"Perhaps." Her gaze flew anxiously to his face. "But he mustn't know that."

He went still. "It's your father who's keeping you here? I thought you said your lover—"

"That's what *you* said." She shook her head. "When would I have time for a relationship? When I'm not in the theater, I'm here."

"Good," he said with satisfaction. "A father should be much easier to deal with than a lover. At least the element of jealousy would be removed."

"A man-woman relationship needn't contain jealousy."

"It needn't, but it often does." He smiled crookedly. "As Shakespeare well knew."

She shivered. "Jealousy is a terrible emotion. I don't understand it."

"I had a few problems with it myself while I was writing *Night Song*." He looked away from her. "I'm beginning to comprehend it a little better now." He changed the subject. "Your father should want the best for you. What kind of a selfish bastard is he to keep you from a chance like this?"

She rounded on him. "He's *not* selfish," she said fiercely. "Charlie would never keep me from anything I wanted to do. He's kind and generous and—"

"Easy." He held up his hand to stop the flow of words. "Sorry. I'm sure he's everything you say he is."

She drew a deep breath. "It's my choice. I can't leave him."

"You're that close?"

She nodded jerkily.

"Charlie?"

"He's actually my stepfather. My mother died when I was five and since then we've had only each other." Her eyes were blazing. "And he's not selfish. He's done everything for me. He loves his work more than anything in the world, but he even gave up painting for five years and took a regular job to be able to afford to have my voice trained by Stoloni."

Jason pounced. "Then he wouldn't want you to sacrifice this chance. He set it up for you."

"Or course not." She looked straight ahead. "And that's why he's not going to know about it."

His gaze was fastened on her face. "I think I may have to have a talk with your father."

"No!" Her hands clenched into fists at her sides. "Haven't you been listening to me? I'd never forgive you if you told him you made me this offer."

"But I might still get what I want," he said coolly. "If your father is as unselfish as you say, he might force you to accept the offer."

She gazed at him, stricken. "You wouldn't do that."

"I want you for Desdemona."

"And it doesn't matter what I want?"

"You want it too." His tone lowered to passionate intensity. "You were meant to play that role. I'll *make* you want it as much as I do."

She stared at him in fascination, captured in the web he was weaving. At that moment she could almost believe that he could make her do anything he wished her to do.

She laughed shakily. "My Lord, are you always this determined?"

"When something is important to me." His demeanor changed as if he had thrown a cloak over that passionate intensity and he grimaced ruefully. "Eric says I'm driven."

"I can believe it. You're very . . . hard."

"And you're very soft." He studied her features. "Idealism and self-sacrifice. You're an anachronism in this world. I think you need someone to save you from yourself."

"By destroying my father's peace of mind?"

"Perhaps we can come to a compromise." Jason smiled faintly. "Suppose we strike a bargain. Give me two weeks."

She gazed at him in bewilderment.

"Let me come here every day and tell you about *Night Song* and my plans for it. In return, I'll give you my promise not to mention my offer to your father."

"It's a waste of time. You won't be able to convince me."

"It's my time." He shrugged. "I can be fairly convincing."

She didn't doubt it. She had already found the force of his personality nearly irresistible. "What if I still say no at the end of that period?"

"Then we're back to square one." He met her gaze. "I won't lie to you. I have no intention of giving up, but you'll have had a two-week grace period."

And two weeks might be enough to convince him she meant what she had said. A man as important as Jason Hayes must have many demands on his time. He might grow bored and impatient long before two weeks and fly back to New York to find another Desdemona.

The sudden pang she experienced at the thought was not pain but relief, she assured herself. "I can't convince you how useless this will be?"

He shook his head.

"All right." She gave in abruptly. "Two weeks." She met his gaze. "But you're not to tell my father your name or anything about who you are. I'll introduce you as a friend I met in Italy. We'll tell him you're connected with the play. You've got to give me your word he won't suspect anything."

His expression was arrested. "And would you trust my word?"

"Yes," she said simply. "You're a hard man, but I don't believe you'd lie to me."

"I see." He held her gaze for a moment. "Trust too. Definitely an anachronism. I think I'll have to hire a bodyguard for you when I get you to New York."

"I'm not going to—"

He interrupted her with a wave of his hand. "We can work that out later. I'll be at your cottage tomorrow morning at ten to—" He stopped, frowning. "No, on second thought, I'll pick you up tonight after the performance. I don't like you driving all this way alone."

"I've done it since the play opened," she reminded him dryly.

"But these are my two weeks. We'll do it my

way." He turned her around and started briskly back the way they had come. "Now, I'll take you back to the cottage to rest. Fantine is a difficult role and it must be taxing."

"Not physically."

"Emotional roles can be even more wearing." He glanced thoughtfully at her. "And you're clearly a woman who gives everything to whatever she does."

There was no hint of sexual innuendo in his tone, and yet she felt a sudden tingling awareness ripple through her. Perhaps she was making a mistake to agree to see him for the next two weeks. She had never experienced this reaction to a man before, and she was going through a vulnerable time.

"You're having second thoughts." He was scanning her face. "Will it help if I tell you that I don't break my promises?"

The knowledge that he had read her so effortlessly only increased her uneasiness.

"Give me my chance." His words came with an odd awkwardness. "It means a hell of a lot to me."

She felt warmth surge through her as she looked at him. She had an idea he wasn't accustomed to pleading for anything, and the expression on his face was endearingly boyish. Who would have guessed she would feel this crazy maternal tenderness for a man like Jason Hayes?

She looked away from him and her pace quickened. "I told you that I'd do it, didn't I?"

He expelled a sigh of relief and lengthened his stride to keep up with her. When he spoke, his tone was carefully careless, "That's right, you did. Just checking."

*   *   *

The phone was ringing when Jason opened the door of his suite two hours later.

"Where the hell have you been?" Eric asked. "I've been—"

Jason cut him short. "What's wrong? Can't you get Bartlin?"

"I haven't had a chance to meet with him yet. We're having lunch tomorrow." Eric paused. "I thought you ought to know Cynthia's here."

Jason stiffened. "In London?"

"She's staying at Claridges."

"How do you know?"

"I went to the theater to check out the box office for the English version of *The Innocents* and Jessup told me she'd stopped by and inquired about you."

"Does she know where I am?"

"Not yet." Eric hesitated. "Before Jessup mentioned she was here I told him you were in Geneva." He added hastily, "But I made him promise not to tell anyone."

A lot of good would that do if Cynthia got her hooks into Jessup, Jason thought wearily. God, he was tired of it all. "Keep in touch with Jessup. When he tells her, I want to know about it."

"Maybe she won't find out, Jason."

He knew better. Cynthia always found out what she wanted to. "Let me know."

Eric muttered a curse half beneath his breath. "Dammit, it's not fair."

"Forget it," Jason said curtly. "When does Peg get there?"

"Tomorrow evening." Eric asked, "Have you signed Daisy Justine yet?"

"I'm working on it. I'll talk to you tomorrow, Eric. Tell Peg I said hello." He hung up the phone and gazed down at it unseeingly. Time was running out. He could feel the frustration searing through him. He had thought he had become resigned to the situation, but it was somehow worse this time.

He started unbuttoning his shirt as he headed for the bathroom. He needed a shower and a drink before he dressed for the theater to see Daisy.

He turned on the shower, adjusted the spray before shedding his clothes. He stepped under the shower and let the warm water run over his body. His muscles were so knotted with tension, they were impervious to the soothing flow. Maybe he should have tried a cold shower. At least the chill might have rid him of the arousal he had been experiencing since seeing Daisy. And lust was only part of it. What the hell was she doing to him?

He closed his eyes, tenderness moving through him in an aching tide as he remembered the way she had looked standing in the sunlight, gazing at him with that wondering expression, so luminous she had seemed part of the sunlight itself. He had wanted to hold her and protect her and—

He reached out with an abrupt hand and turned off the water. It wasn't tenderness, it was a mere sexual obsession. She was a different type and her resistance had sparked his libido. It wasn't tenderness.

He couldn't let it be tenderness.

Jason was waiting in the alley at the stage door when Daisy came down the concrete steps that evening. Her heart gave a leap, and she tried not to let him see the sudden happiness she felt at the mere sight of him. "I told you this wasn't necessary. I have my own car and I'll need it to get to the theater tomorrow."

"No, you won't." He took her arm and propelled her down the alley toward the street. "No problem. From now on I'll drive you back and forth every day." He opened the passenger door of the dark blue Mercedes parked at the curb. "I'll have someone from the hotel pick up your car and drive it to your home tomorrow."

She cast him an exasperated glance as she got into the car.

He grimaced. "I've irritated you again."

"I'm used to doing things for myself."

He went around the car and slid into the driver's seat. "I . . . like doing things for you."

Again she sensed that uncharacteristic awkwardness in him and again she found herself melting. "I believe we may have to have a few discussions on the principles of women's lib."

"I'm not usually a chauvinist." He looked straight ahead as he put the car in gear and pulled away from the curb. "This is different. I want to protect you. I *need* to protect you."

She looked at him, puzzled.

He didn't elaborate but changed the subject. "I didn't think it was possible, but you were even better tonight than you were last night."

"You were in the audience?"

He nodded. "But I don't think I'll go again."

She smiled understandingly. "I suppose you've seen the play so many times it must bore you to tears."

"Music never bores me." His hands tightened on the steering wheel. "It's you."

"What?"

He laughed harshly. "I'm jealous. I thought I was only caught off balance the other night but it happened again tonight." He shook his head. "Crazy."

"I don't know what you're talking about."

He glanced sidewise at her, his pale eyes shimmering in the light of the dashboard. "I didn't want to share you. I wanted the experience to be all *mine*."

Shock went through her and the breath left her body.

"I've scared you." He muttered a curse. "Now you think I'm some kind of nut. Hell, maybe I am."

She said carefully, "I suppose I should be flattered."

"But you still think I'm a nut." He made a face. "It's all right, I've been thinking the same thing about myself. This has never happened to me before. I've been trying to tell myself that it's just your voice."

Her gaze flew to his face. "Of course it's my voice."

He shook his head, his gaze returning to the street. "Only partly." He paused. "It's sexual." He heard her sharp intake of breath and the glance he shot her was like a blue-green lance. "You can't be surprised. You knew it was there."

Yes, she knew. The sexual chemistry had been present from the first moment she had seen him. "There's an . . . attraction."

"It's more than an attraction. It's damn near kinetic."

She swallowed. "I don't want an affair with you."

"That makes two of us. So what do we do?"

"Ignore it." Her hands clenched on the strap of her shoulderbag. "You could go back to New York."

"No way." He smiled lopsidedly. "And you're wrong, I can't ignore it. Do you know what I've been thinking since you got in the car?"

She shook her head. "And I don't want to know."

"I've been thinking how much I'd like you to unbutton that silk blouse and let me look at your breasts."

Her eyes widened as a hot tide suffused her and she murmured a soft protest as his gaze moved down her throat to the rise of her breasts.

"I've been thinking how ruby-colored your nipples might be in the light of the dashboard. I've been thinking how I'd like you to come over here and let me fondle you as I drive. I've been thinking how much I'd like to pull over to the side of the road and take off—"

"Stop." Her voice was trembling and she tried to steady it. "We're not a couple of teenagers."

"I never felt like this when I was a teenager," he said thickly. "I told you it was new to me." He forced his gaze back to the road. "Will you come back to the hotel with me?"

"No."

He muttered a curse. "Dammit, you want it."

"I don't do one-night stands."

"It's the only way we're going to get rid of it. It wouldn't be an affair. No strings. Just let me—"

"No!" She tried to keep her voice from shaking.

"I'm not an animal. Besides, it would complicate everything. I can't deal with this right now."

"Do you think I can?" He pulled over to the side of the road and turned off the car. He sat hunched over the steering wheel, his knuckles turning white as he gripped the smooth plastic. "Look, it *has* to happen. You have to play Desdemona and I can't keep on feeling this—" He stopped searching for words. "Sense of possession. Maybe if we—"

"Oh, I see." They were speaking of lust, not any gentler emotion, and she shouldn't feel so hurt. Yet her tone sounded brittle even to herself. "You think if we hop into bed you'll be able to look at me with more perspective. What a charming way to put it. I believe I prefer your music to your lyrics."

"I'm trying to be honest. Do you think it's easy for me?" He looked straight ahead. "Come with me. I'm not particularly kinky. I promise I'd make it good for you."

"I think you'd better take me home."

He muttered an imprecation beneath his breath and turned on the ignition.

The rest of the drive was made in silence, but the air in the car was so heavily charged with emotion, Daisy found it hard to breathe.

The lights were ablaze in the cottage when Jason pulled over to the curb. "Does your father always wait up for you?"

"He keeps late hours. He's probably working." She reached for the handle of the door. "Good night."

"Wait." He put his hand on her arm, and a bittersweet smile curved his lips as he heard her gasp at this touch. "You see? I can't lay a hand on you without us both going up in flames." His hand moved to touch her throat and then moved down to finger the top button of her blouse. She could feel the warmth of his knuckles on her upper breast through the thin silk. Her breasts were swelling, pushing against the material, and the muscles of her belly instinctively clenched. She knew she should break the spell and get out of the car, but she couldn't seem to move.

He slipped the pearl button from the hole, and his index finger slowly rubbed up and down on the flesh of her cleavage. She looked down at the contrast of his tanned hand against the delicate silk of her blouse, the pale gleam of her breast under his finger. He said softly, "It's going to happen, Daisy."

His finger slipped into her bra and touched her nipple. She bit her lower lip to smother her cry as he rubbed back and forth on the aroused, distended tip. A liquid aching was starting between her thighs. She wanted to lean toward him, she wanted to shrug out of the blouse and pull his mouth down to—

"No!" She opened the door and got out of the car. "The hell it is. Our agreement had nothing to do with sex."

"But what's between us has everything to do with sex. If you'd come with me, we might eventually be able to see the woods for the trees."

She stood on the sidewalk, looking at him. "Please," she whispered. "I don't want to be in your play. I don't want to see you again."

"Don't worry. I'm not going to push it. I guess I knew it was too soon, but I'm running out of time."

"Running out of time?"

"Never mind." He switched on the ignition. "I'll see you tomorrow."

"No."

He frowned. "There's nothing to be frightened about. I'm no rapist. I'll wait until you come to me."

She wasn't afraid he'd use force. She didn't fear him so much as the magnetism drawing them together. "It's not a good idea. I've got problems enough without—"

"Then let me solve them."

"In return for a romp in the hay?"

He flinched as if she had struck him. "I'm not a complete bastard. I told you I wanted to help you."

"To clear my way to play your Desdemona?"

"No, it's more than that."

"I don't believe you."

"I know you don't." He shrugged wearily. "I'll be here at noon tomorrow."

She gazed at him helplessly before turning on her heel and striding toward the cottage. A moment later the door of the cottage slammed behind her.

Charlie stood at the easel across the room and didn't look up. "I'm glad you're home. This damn still life is frustrating the hell out of me. Are you too tired to pose?"

Sweet heaven, she didn't want to pose tonight. She was raw, burning, yearning. . . . She wanted nothing more than to shut herself in her room and go to bed and let the blessed oblivion of sleep obscure those moments in the car with Jason.

Charlie didn't look up. "Daisy?"

She wasn't a sex-crazy adolescent. She had to come to terms with this magnetism Jason held for her. She couldn't hide from what she felt and had no right to self-indulgence when she had such a great responsibility to Charlie. "I'm not tired." She smiled gently at him. "Just let me go change and comb my hair and I'll be right with you."

Daisy was waiting on the doorstep the next morning when Jason's car pulled up to the curb. She instinctively tensed as she watched him get out of the car and come toward her. He was dressed in faded jeans, brown leather moccasins, and a jade-green cotton sweater and looked completely different from the elegant man who had left her last night. He might have been one of the unassuming young artists who lived in St. Genève. No, she was wrong. As he drew closer she could sense his controlled power that could never be lessened by the casualness of his clothes.

He raised his black brows. "Are you guarding the gate?"

"I thought about what you said last night after I went to bed. It's not logical that it's me you're really attracted to. I'm not the type of woman men develop fixations on." She rushed on. "And I decided it was Desdemona."

He looked at her blankly.

"Don't you see? You have me mixed up with Desdemona in your mind."

"Indeed?"

She nodded. "You're a sensitive, creative person, and naturally you'd identify with the characters in a play you've worked on for so long."

"Sensitive?" The word sounded sour on his tongue. "Lord, I hate that word. I grew up in a rough neighborhood in the Bronx and do you know how many noses I bloodied when I was a kid to prove I wasn't 'sensitive'?"

She didn't know much about him at all, she realized. She had a sudden vision of Jason, totally absorbed with his music and yet struggling for a normal boyhood among his peers. She felt a rush of sympathy. "Oh, dear, it must have been terrible for you."

"I survived." He studied her softened expression and misty eyes and wonderingly shook his head. "Just look at you, I tell you a hard luck story and you melt. Lord, you're easy. You'd never have lasted five minutes in the Bronx."

She bristled. "It's not soft to feel sympathy. Maybe if you'd tried to reason with those kids instead of bloodying their noses, you'd have had an easier time of it."

He smiled. "If you say so." He paused. "So you think I want to go to bed with you because you're Desdemona. Why do you want to go to bed with me? Do you see me as Othello?"

"I wasn't talking about me," she said hurriedly.

"Sure you were." His brows knitted in a frown. "Let's see, I understand Othello, but we're not that much alike. I'm too selfish to kill the woman I loved." His smile gleamed tiger-bright. "I would have killed her lover and then found another way to punish her."

"Listen to me." She was losing control of the conversation. "Once you accept that I'm not going to be Desdemona, you'll probably no longer find me appealing."

He smiled curiously. "Go on."

"I thought we'd go for a walk in the hills. You can tell me about the play."

"I see." He snapped his fingers. "I try to convince you to play the part. You refuse me. I'm immediately rid of this fixation I have on you and toddle on my way. Is that the scenario?" He shook his head and for an instant a flicker of tenderness crossed his face. "Sorry, love, it's too simplistic. Just what I would have expected of you."

She flushed. "I'm not simple."

"Yes, you are," he said quietly. "You have a lovely glowing simplicity of spirit that I've never seen before." He held up his hand when she opened her lips to speak. "I'm not insulting you. I've never equated simplicity with stupidity. You're obviously intelligent, if a little muddle-headed."

She couldn't look away from him. Tenderness, humor, sadness, were all there in his expression. She was seeing dimensions she hadn't known existed in Jason Hayes and had a urgent desire to see more, deeper. She stepped down from the stoop and started along the walk toward the gate. "Shall we go?"

"No."

She looked back at him, startled.

"I stayed awake last night and made a few decisions too." He smiled. "Though I can't claim it was because I was clinically taking apart our situation. I was randy as hell and hurting." He turned back toward the cottage. "And I decided I wasn't going to make it easy for you to get rid of me." He reached for the knob of the door.

"No!" She hurried back up the walk, but he had already opened the door and was striding into the cottage.

"Mr. Justine?" Jason moved across the room toward Charlie. "I'm Jason Link. Perhaps Daisy's told you about me?"

Relief rushed through her. Link, not Hayes. He wasn't going to break his promise to her.

Charlie looked up with a puzzled frown. "I don't believe she has, Mr. Link." His gaze went inquiringly to Daisy. "I didn't know you were expecting company, Daisy. I thought you were going for a walk alone."

"I guess I forget to mention Jason."

"I'm devastated," Jason said lightly as he held out his hand to Charlie. "I've heard a lot about you, Mr. Justine. You must be quite a man to earn a devotion like Daisy's."

Charlie shook Jason's hand. "I'm a lucky man," he said simply. "Where did you meet Daisy, Mr. Link?"

"Jason. We knew each other in Milan, and I joined the company two weeks ago."

"You're a singer?"

Jason grimaced. "You wouldn't ask that if you heard me in the shower. I'm a pianist in the orchestra."

Charlie's sandy brows lifted in surprise. "I thought they already had a pianist."

"It's only a part-time job so far. I fill in on vacations and weekends."

"I see." Charlie's gaze shifted again to Daisy. "I'm glad to meet you, Mr. Link. Daisy rarely brings anyone home. I'm afraid I've been selfish and kept her pretty much to myself for the past year or so."

"Nonsense." Daisy came into the room and closed the door. "I'm the one who has been selfish."

"I like this room." Jason's gaze flicked from the faded beige and cream-colored chintz upholstery of the couch and matching easy chair to the colorful rugs scattered on the pine floor and then to the breakfast bar separating the central living area from the adjoining kitchenette. "It's cozy."

Charlie smiled lopsidedly. "A euphemism for tiny."

"No." Jason met Charlie's gaze. "I say what I mean. It's a home." He moved toward the ancient upright piano against the wall. "I used to have one of these in my apartment in Queens."

"You're a New Yorker?"

Jason nodded. "Born and bred." Jason strolled over and examined the picture Charlie was working on. "Daisy." He tilted his head. "I think you've caught her."

Charlie's blue eyes lit with eagerness. "It's the best thing I've ever done."

"No fair," Daisy protested. "He won't let me take even a peek at it."

Jason smiled faintly, still staring at the painting. "I can see why." He glanced at Charlie. "Don't let me interrupt you."

"I was only working on the background. I need Daisy to pose to work on the figure." His gaze drifted wistfully back to the painting. "Perhaps when you come back from your walk . . ."

"Why not now?" Jason gestured for Daisy to mount the platform. "I'm not up to a mountain trek today. The two of you just go on and do what you'd ordinarily do and I'll wander around the cottage and watch. I've never seen an artist at work."

Charlie frowned doubtfully. "Are you sure?"

"I'm sure." Jason's smile was surprisingly gentle as he gazed at the older man. "Paint her. She's evidently one hell of an inspiring subject." He turned and headed for the kitchenette. "You don't mind if I make myself at home? I'll make coffee for us while genius burns and then maybe play you some mood music."

"Just as long as it's not heavy metal."

"I'll make the coffee," Daisy said.

He glanced at her over his shoulder. "And waste your father's painting time? We'll have to leave for the theater in a few hours." He went into the kitchenette and began opening cabinets. "Let me make the coffee."

Daisy gazed at him uncertainly. Jason had swept into the cottage, charmed Charlie, and insinuated himself into their household all in the space of a few moments.

"If you'd rather not . . ." Charlie said hesitantly. "I know it's not what you planned."

"No, it's fine." She mounted the platform and sat down in the chair, her gaze still on Jason moving about in the kitchenette. "I don't mind."

Jason's behavior during the next few hours astonished Daisy. Somehow he managed to cloak that bigger-than-life aura clinging to him and became both appealing and unassuming. He made coffee and served it to them, sat down at the piano and played a few Chopin selections. Then he settled himself cross-legged on the floor before the platform and watched silently as the hours passed. Only when Charlie stopped work did he start a casual conversation that lasted until it was time for her to dress to go to the theater.

"I like him," Charlie whispered to Daisy before she walked out the door. "Bring him back."

"We'll see." She kissed him lightly on the cheek and followed Jason from the cottage to the Mercedes at the curb.

"You're frowning." Jason held the passenger

door of the car open for her. "I thought I'd behaved rather well."

"I don't like deceiving Charlie."

"It was your idea."

"I know, but you didn't have to—"

"Look." He gazed directly at her. "I like your stepfather. The only phony baloney I handed out back there was the story you wanted me to tell him. The rest was strictly on the up and up."

"Really?"

He smiled and nodded. "He reminded me of my first piano teacher. A little gentler, maybe. I don't think he'd hit my knuckles with a ruler if I struck a wrong key."

"No, Charlie wouldn't hurt anyone."

"And neither would you." His face softened as he resignedly shook his head. "What a pair."

She felt a strange sudden warmth deep inside her as she watched him go around the car and get in the driver's seat. "I don't think you're as cynical as you'd like me to believe."

He shrugged. "Maybe it's infectious. I assure you I'm not like this with anyone else." He started the car and edged away from the curb. "But since you evidently think I'm not completely beyond redemption, perhaps you'll relax the next time I'm in the same room with Charlie. You were on edge the entire time I was there. You told me once you thought I could be trusted. I don't think I've done anything today to change that, have I?"

She gazed at him silently for a moment and again felt that curiously sweet warmth flowering within her. "No," she said softly. "You haven't done anything today to change that."

Three

"This is my favorite place." Daisy sighed contentedly as she sat down on the grass and looked out over snowcapped mountains and then to the village in the valley below. "Isn't the view spectacular?"

"Wait a minute until I stop wheezing and I'll tell you." Jason dropped down beside her and leaned back against the boulder. "You didn't warn me when we started out that I'd have to climb a mountain to get to this view."

"Only a small mountain. It's scarcely more than a hill." She glanced at him anxiously and then relaxed when she saw he wasn't even out of breath. "You're joking?"

He smiled faintly his gaze on her face. "Very perceptive."

"But isn't it worth the climb?" She threw her arm out in an expansive gesture. "Isn't it wonderful?"

"Radiant." His stare was still fixed on her face. He shifted his gaze to the valley below. "The view's good too."

42

She flushed and felt a moment of awkwardness. It was the first time in the past week Jason had said anything that could be termed personal. She had been conscious of the undercurrent of sexuality, but it had been like music played far away that she could catch a chord of only now and then.

"Don't draw away from me." He was still looking at the valley. "I thought we were good enough friends for me not to have to watch every word."

She was being foolish. They *were* friends. She would never have believed she could become friends with Jason Hayes after their tumultuous start, but somehow it had happened. During the past days she had found him to be amusing and clever with a wry sense of humor that was often directed at himself. He had practically moved into the cottage, and he and Charlie were drawing closer every day. A few evenings he had even driven back to the cottage to spend the evening with her father after he had dropped her off at the theater.

"Sorry." She smiled and relaxed. "I had a flashback to that first night you came backstage. You intimidated me."

"But I don't now?"

She shook her head. "That wasn't really you. Actually, you're very kind."

He raised his brows. "I don't know if I feel flattered or insulted. I rather like being intimidating."

She chuckled. "Well, you blew it."

His smile disappeared and his eyes glinted ice-green as he asked softly, "Is that a challenge?"

She felt a sudden heat, a fluttering along her nerve endings. "No."

"It's still there, you know," he said quietly.

"Just as strong, just as fierce. Except I'm keeping it under wraps for a while." He paused. "Only a warning—between friends."

She was suddenly acutely conscious of the physical presence of the man sitting beside her. The wind lifting Jason's dark hair away from his face, the sunlight on his tanned skin, the way the soft fabric of his faded jeans molded the brawny muscles of his thighs, the power and strength of his hands.

She swallowed and quickly glanced out at the valley again. She sought wildly for a change of subject. "I liked your brother. The two of you aren't very much alike."

He was silent an instant, as if deciding whether or not to accept the sidestep, and finally said, "I know. Eric says I'm a throwback to an Apache great-grandfather," Jason said. "My brother got all the charm and business sense and all I got was a muse whispering in my ear and tormenting the hell out of me."

"But you wouldn't change places?"

"No, my music's everything." For a moment his voice was bitter. "It has to be."

"What do you mean?"

"Just what I said." He changed the subject. "It's no wonder your projection is so good, that your voice completely fills the theater. All this climbing must give you great lungs."

"It helps and the exercise keeps me from getting stressed out." She wrinkled her nose. "Fantine's never been an easy role for me."

"Why not?"

"Because I've been so lucky," she said simply. "Fantine suffered disillusion, desertion by her lover, separation from her child, loss of everything that made life worth living. It's hard for me to identify with her." She picked up a blade of grass and chewed it thoughtfully. "God gave me my voice, and that was a special joy, and then he topped it off by giving me loving parents. I haven't suffered enough to play Fantine well."

"You lost your mother."

"But Charlie was right there bolstering me, supporting me." She added softly, "Loving me." She gazed absently down into the valley. "Do you know that line from Fantine's song. 'But the tigers came at night?' "

"Yes."

"Well, the tigers have never come to me." She laughed shakily. "Yet." She glanced curiously at him. "Have they come to you, Jason?"

"Oh, yes." He drew up his knees and looped his arms around them. "By night and by day."

"I'm sorry."

He nodded. "I know you are." His gaze lifted to her face. "I wish I could tell you that they will never come to you, but they come to all of us eventually."

"I'm not so naive I don't realize that." She closed her eyes and shivered as she whispered, "Lord, sometimes I get so scared."

He went still. "What's wrong, Daisy?"

For an instant she was desperately tempted to tell him. They had become very close in many ways during these past few days, and sometimes she felt so alone in her waiting that it would have been an enormous comfort to confide in someone. But she couldn't take the easy way. She had promised Charlie, and it might be the last promise he would ever ask of her. Her eyes flicked open and she smiled with an effort. "Nothing. I was only telling you why Fantine was difficult for me."

His gaze narrowed on her face. "No, it's more than that."

She scrambled to her feet. "It's time we went back to the cottage. Since I don't have a performance tonight, I promised I'd spend the evening posing for Charlie." She dusted the seat of her jeans and started down the path. "Don't worry, it's much easier going down."

"Why won't you talk to me?"

"I could ask you the same thing." She met his gaze directly. "You never really talk about yourself. The tabloids are right. You're the original mystery man."

His expression became guarded. "There's not much to tell."

"You can't expect confidences if you don't return them."

He smiled crookedly. "And what if I opened my jaded soul to you?"

She hesitated, her gaze on his face. He was one of the most complicated and fascinating men she had ever met, and she suddenly realized she desperately wanted to know what circumstances had molded the man who was Jason Hayes.

But not if it mean betraying her word to Charlie.

He read her answer in her expression. "I didn't think you were in the market for a trade." He shrugged. "All right, fair is fair. We'll consider this a hiatus. No questions asked."

She started to turn away.

"Daisy."

She glanced back to see him still sitting where she had left him.

"Let me know when your tigers come and I'll help you fight them."

She shook her head. "When they come, I'll have to fight them myself." She smiled. "Just as you did."

He rose to his feet. "Let me know anyway."

"Maybe." A sudden hollowness echoed through her as she remembered that their time together was almost over. "If you're around."

"I'll be arou—" He broke off and was silent for a long moment. "I'll find a way to reach you." He started down the path after her. "Call me."

"It's no good!" Charlie threw down the brush and turned away from the easel. "I don't know why I try. It's no damn good."

Daisy stood up and jumped down from the platform. "What's wrong? You were so pleased with it."

"Because I'm a fool." Charlie's face was tormented. "Because I lie to myself."

"I like it, Charlie." Jason stood up from the piano he had been softly playing for the last hour. "And I don't consider myself a fool."

"You like it because it's Daisy," Charlie said harshly. "Do you think I don't know that? I'm as tired of your lies as I am of my own." He strode across the room and slammed out of the cottage.

"Shall I go after him?" Jason asked.

"No, leave him alone. He doesn't like company when he's like this." Daisy folded her arms across her chest to stop the trembling. She felt as raw and broken as if Charlie's torment were her own. "He explodes now and then. It's artistic temperament. He'll go for a long walk, stop at a bar and have a few drinks, and then come home. He'll be okay by the time he gets back. He's going through a bad time now."

"Can I help?"

She shook her head. "Tell me, is his portrait of me any good?"

Jason hesitated. "I'm no art critic."

Daisy sighed. "It's not good."

"I didn't say that. I don't know about the technical side, but it's full of emotion, it's full of . . . love."

Daisy felt the tears sting her eyes. "Yes, he's very good at love." Her eyes were jewel-bright as she gazed at him across the room. "It's not fair, you know. All his life he's wanted only one thing, to create something truly beautiful, to create something special. You'd think he would have been allowed that—" Her voice broke. "He's such a good man, Jason."

"I know," he said gently. "Charlie's a great guy. I like him very much."

Suddenly she couldn't take it any longer. The waiting had gone on too long and the world seemed full of pain and injustice. She had to run away from it before it overwhelmed her.

"Come on." She snatched up the fringed shawl and headed for the door. "We can't stay here waiting for him. It will only make him feel guilty when he comes back."

"Where are we going?"

"For a drive . . . no, for a walk. I need the exercise. I feel as if I'm about to explode. The mountain. I think I'll go to the mountain."

"It's dark out."

"That won't bother me. I know the path."

"For Lord's sake, at least change clothes. The soles of those slippers won't grip the—"

"I don't care. I need to go *now*." She whirled at the door to look at him, trying to keep her voice steady. "I know I'm behaving like an idiot. You don't have to come with me."

"Don't be stupid," he said roughly. "Of course I'm coming with you."

She led the way up the mountain at a fast pace, trying not to think of anything but putting one foot before the other, to stretch her endurance to the limit so that she wouldn't think of Charlie's tormented expression before he left the cottage.

By the time she reached the summit, the blood was pounding in her veins, her head was swimming, and her lungs ached with every breath.

She stood on the summit and looked down at the lights of the houses in the valley. Charlie was probably in the bar by now, talking quietly to the bartender, sipping his beer, feeling discouraged and—

But she couldn't think of Charlie right now. It hurt too much.

She turned to Jason, who was climbing the last few yards. "Look at the moonlight on the lake," she said. "I don't like moonlight as much as sunlight, but I can't deny it's effective. What is there about light on water? Poets talk about it. Ballets are choreographed to extol its beauties. You'd think that—"

"Hush." Jason's breath was coming harshly, but the word was enunciated with precision. "You're babbling and it's not like you."

"Babble is a water word too." Even to herself

her tone sounded feverish and the words kept welling, spilling out into the night. "You're very good at words. I've often thought your lyrics strike a chord in all of us."

He gripped her shoulders and shook her. "What the hell is wrong with you? I know you're upset about Charlie, but you're overreacting."

"Am I?" She turned to look out over the mountain range and in panic felt the emptiness rushing back to her. "You're probably right, but there are moments when it's—" She suddenly buried her face in his chest. "Will you make love to me, Jason?"

She felt him grow tense. "What?"

She was surprised as he was at her question. It had come out of nowhere, born of her sadness and desperation. Yet, in spite of her shock and the surge of tremulous fear that followed, she wasn't sorry for the words. Jason could help her, Jason could ease the pain and push away the approaching darkness.

"I mean it. I want to feel *alive*. I want to forget—" She broke off and lifted her head to stare up at him. "You said that . . . well, maybe you don't want me anymore. I understand if you don't want to do it."

"Oh, I want to do it all right," he said dryly. "I'm ready to pull you down to the ground and take you. But I don't know if I can."

"Why not? I said I wanted to do it."

"I find I have a few scruples left." His expression was grim in the moonlight. "For some reason you're practically shell-shocked."

She pressed closer and buried her face in his soft black cashmere sweater. She could hear the vibration of his heart beneath her ear and felt the waves of heat emitting from his big body. Life. Safety from the threat of the tigers. "I'm fine."

"The hell you are," he said hoarsely.

She could feel his arousal pressing against her, his muscles tensing, ready. "I *need* you."

His heartbeat accelerated. "I believe you do." He paused. "Here?"

Her own heart gave a wild leap, and she kept her cheek pressed to his chest. "Yes. Right here, right now. Will you do it?"

"If I was a nice guy like Eric, I'd say no." He pushed her away and smiled recklessly down at her. "But what the hell? I'm no angel, and I've always been one to take advantage of the moment. Lord knows we may never have anything else." He pulled his sweater over his head and dropped it on the ground beside them. "I've wanted you too much to be choosy about the way I get you." He unbuttoned his shirt, stripped it off, and dropped it on top of the sweater. "Take off your gown."

Her aggressiveness vanished and she felt suddenly shy. She stood staring at him with blazing cheeks.

"Shall I do it?" He didn't wait for an answer as he took a step closer and began to unfasten the tiny buttons marching down her bodice. "It's strange how a period gown like this makes a man feel."

"How does it—" She gasped as his knuckles brushed the inner swelling of her breasts as his fingers deftly negotiated the buttons.

"Like a brigand from another age," he said softly. "One who had no rules when he wanted a woman. All those hours I sat there in the cottage and watched your father paint you and thought about how I'd like to do this. I began to have all kinds of fantasies." He undid the last button, his gaze on her breasts tumbling from the loosened bodice. "About how I'd take off your gown and sit down in that big chair on the platform with you on my lap. How I'd like to put you astride me and rub you against me." He parted the material of her bodice and looked at the full globes of her breasts. His breath expelled in a burst of air. "Damn."

She couldn't breathe and she was trembling uncontrollably. The summer wind touched her taut nipples but she felt no cooling. The eroticism of his words was as much an aphrodisiac as his gaze on her body.

His big, warm palms cupped her breasts.

Her teeth bit into her lower lip to keep from crying out.

His gaze held her own as he squeezed and released, squeezed and released, rhythmically, gently, possessively. "I thought how you'd like it. How you'd squirm and move against me." His head lowered and his mouth enveloped her nipple. He sucked strongly, pumping her, his teeth pulling at her. "How you'd let me do anything I wanted to you."

Her spine arched backward and she moaned softly.

"Wouldn't you?" he muttered. "Tell me."

She couldn't make sense of his words; she was lost in heat and sensation.

"Tell me."

"Yes . . ."

He drew her closer and the warm, naked flesh of his chest and the triangle of dark hair was a sensual shock against her nipples. Another moan broke from her as he slowly rubbed her back and forth against his body. "Yes, that's right," he said thickly. "Feel me. *Know* me." His hands left her hips and moved to her hair, loosening the combs that held it in place. It flowed around her, and his fingers tangled in its soft thickness. "Your hair . . . I've wanted to do this so many times . . . I want to wrap it around me, drown in it, drown in you." He stripped her quickly, feverishly pushing her down on the ground. The grass was cool against her nakedness, the scent of earth and growth surrounded her.

Life, again. The night was brimming, burning with vibrant life, and she wanted to hold on to it, all of it, before it slipped away.

He stood looking down at her, quickly shedding the rest of his own garments. "Let me look at you. Open your legs," he begged hoarsely.

She slowly parted her thighs, and she could feel his gaze on her womanhood, vulnerable to him. The muscles of her stomach clenched and she felt her breasts swell as she looked up at him. He was a giant male, overwhelming, and she had never felt more exposed than in this erotic, submissive position.

He fell to his knees and moved between her thighs. His palms pressed down on her diaphragm, throwing her breasts into greater prominence but not touching them. But she wanted to be touched, she thought dazedly. She wanted to be devoured, absorbed by him.

"Do you want me?" he asked hoarsely. "If you don't, say so now. There's no going back once you belong to me. Hell, I don't think I'll be able to maintain control once I start."

Belong. For an instant she felt a frisson of

apprehension at the possessiveness of the word.
Othello. This wasn't the wry, clever man who had
become her friend in the last week. In the moonlight he was all fierce, sensual warrior.

He leaned forward and his warm tongue touched
her belly.

"Quick," he muttered. "Neither of us can wait.
Do you want me inside you?" He moved up, nudg-
ing against her but not entering her. *"Do you
want me?"*

She was burning up, dizzy with need and reck-
lessness-banished caution. "Yes. Oh, yes."

He plunged forward, burying himself in the
depths of her.

She cried out and her spine arched upward.
Fullness, thickness, warmth. "Jason!"

He froze. "Lord, why didn't you tell me? Did I
hurt you?" His teeth clenched. "Stupid. Of course
I hurt you."

"No, it's . . ." Her hands closed on the grass.
"I'm— Oh, please, go on!"

His expression was tortured. "It's too late to do
anything else. I can't stop. I'll try to go easy," he
said thickly. "I just had to be part of you." He
drew out and then back, establishing a slow
rhythm. "You took me. All of me. See how well we
fit? Can you feel me?"

Every inch, every texture. Her fingernails dug
into the earth. "Yes."

"Do you like it?" His hips moved in a circular
motion and she gasped as he invaded new depths.
"I want you to love it." He forgot gentleness and
began plunging wildly, strongly, deeply. "Moan for
me. Let me hear you. I want it all."

She *was* moaning. She couldn't help herself.
She lunged upward, trying to match his pace, try-

ing to keep up with him, but he was too wild, too strong, too stallion-hot. She could only hold on to him and let him ride her. Her head thrashed back and forth on the grass as his hands went around and cupped her buttocks, lifting her into each powerful thrust.

Tension was mounting. She could her voice begging, pleading with him for more. His chest lifted in and out with each harsh breath as he moved, his light eyes glittering wildly in the moonlit darkness, his features set as if he were in pain.

"Give to me." His teeth were set, his eyes half closed. "Now!"

The tension broke and the release was as earth-shaking as what had gone before. He cried out and clutched her close, almost bruising her with the force of his grip.

It was a moment before he stirred, and when he lifted his head, another shock awaited her. The passion was gone and his expression . . .

Tenderness, wonder, vulnerability. He lifted his hand and stroked her tousled fair hair back from her face with the most exquisite gentleness. "Okay?"

She nodded, her gaze clinging to his face. Here was a more sensitive, gentler Jason Hayes, a man she had somehow sensed was there behind the hard façade but never seen. She felt strange—warm, glowing, filled with joy and . . . and something else. What? Whatever that emotion was, it was just out of reach, lost in the mists formed by the haze of satiated passion enfolding them.

He pulled her hair over her shoulders and draped it over her breasts. Then he laid his cheek on the silky pillow and rubbed slowly back and forth. "Another fantasy," he murmured. "Lord, you have beautiful hair." He dropped an affectionate kiss on one nipple poking through the strands. "Among other equally lovely aspects of your anatomy."

Her nipple tightened in response, and he smiled in delight and his lips slowly lowered to hover just above it. "This one I find positively enchanting." He blew on the distended tip and smiled again as it hardened. "Daisy my love, you may look like an angel, but you definitely have the instincts of a voluptuary."

My love. For some odd reason the light words hurt her. "Aren't you going to get off me?"

"It seems a waste of time. Besides, I like it here."

She liked it too. His weight seemed so wonderfully right on her body. "We have to get back. Charlie . . ."

His smile faded. "Ah, yes, the world intrudes." He moved off her and to the side. "Are you going to tell me what this is all about now? I was hardly expecting a virgin to seduce me." His lips twisted. "Hell, I wasn't expecting a virgin at all. For heaven's sake, you're twenty-four years old."

She felt lonely without him. She wanted him back. "I have a career. I've been busy. You didn't seem to mind at the time."

His gaze moved over her possessively. "Hell no. I . . . liked it." He reached out to touch her hair and then stopped, and his hand fell to his side. "But I don't flatter myself that I was the reason you suddenly decided it was time to change your virginal condition. I wasn't even trying to arouse you."

A man with Jason's virile appeal didn't have to

try, she thought ruefully. All he had to be was himself. "I don't know what you mean."

"I think you do." His expression was no longer vulnerable but guarded once again. "I didn't sweep you off your feet tonight, but *something* sure as hell did."

She stiffened, rolled away from him and sat up. "It's pretty obvious, isn't it?" she asked lightly. "You said yourself our chemistry was kinetic. You're a very attractive man. I'm surprised I held out this long."

"Bull." His answer was bluntly succinct. "Dammit, something's wrong."

She stood up and began to dress. "Of course there was something wrong. I was upset about Charlie."

"Why?" His gaze searched her face. "You said yourself he'd be okay by the time he came home."

"Yes, he'll be fine." She pulled on her gown and quickly fastened the bodice before thrusting her feet into the black ballet slippers. She looked around on the ground, but she couldn't find the combs Jason had taken from her hair so she ran her fingers through her hair to tidy it. "But it's time I got back to him."

"Not yet." He stayed where he was on the grass. "Talk to me."

"I told you—" She stopped and reached down to pick up her shawl from the grass. "Why are you interrogating me? You told me yourself that sex would be a form of therapy. What did you say? 'Just a romp in the hay to get it out of our systems.' No strings and—"

"Dammit, those were your words and you know it's not like that now." His voice was harsh with exasperation. "I care about you. I want to help you. Why won't you talk to me?"

"There's nothing to say."

His smile held a touch of bitterness. "You could tell me why you used me."

The word shocked her. "I didn't use you." She knew as soon as she said it that it wasn't the truth. She had used him to hold away the pain, but she hadn't meant to. "Perhaps I did. But no more than you used me."

He stood up and began to dress. "Did you feel used, Daisy?"

She remembered that moment when he had touched her cheek with exquisite tenderness and the joy and wonder it had brought. She had felt swept away, treasured, possessed. Used? Never.

"No." The night chill was beginning to reach her now that she was no longer touching him. She took a step back and wrapped the fringed shawl around her. "Can we go back now?"

For an instant she thought she saw a flicker of hurt in his expression, and then it was gone. "Sure." He pulled his crew-necked sweater over his head and settled it about his hips. "Why not?" He gestured mockingly toward the path. "After you."

She opened her lips to speak and then closed them and started down the path.

His soft words followed her. "But you should know this is the last time I let you lead the way. From now on I'm on the initiative."

She glanced at him warily over her shoulder. "What do you mean?"

He smiled crookedly. "I mean, one time wasn't enough. Not for either of us. It's going to take more than once to do the job." He paused. "I mean I'm going to get you into the sack at the earliest possible convenience and repeat the experience over and over and over."

She felt the breath leave her body. "I don't think—"

"Don't worry, I have no intention of any major interference in your life. I'll take what I can get. Now. All I ask is that you come to my room at the hotel every night after the performance. We can spend a few hours indulging ourselves in pleasure, and then I'll take you home." He lifted his brows quizzically. "I trust you're in agreement?"

She gazed at him uncertainly even as a reminiscent tingling started between her thighs. Their lovemaking had been so powerful, she was still trembling from it, and there was no question she wanted him again. What would it be like when they learned each other's bodies and knew how to please each other? She would probably be foolish to pursue a path that led to sensual addiction. Dear heaven, she wasn't sure she wasn't already on that path.

Yet, she *needed* him. For those moments in his arms she had forgotten everything but the pleasure he was giving her. She needed that release if she was going to make it through the weeks ahead. He had made it clear he wanted no permanent commitment, but there was no reason she shouldn't take the comfort he could give her. "I . . . don't know. I'll have to think about it." She started down the rock-strewn path again.

"One more thing."

He was still smiling, but she could sense a hardness in him she hadn't seen since those first days of their acquaintance. "Desdemona," he said. "I'm not going to lie to you. I still intend to get you for Desdemona."

The golden hiatus was over, the challenge was thrown down.

She silently shook her head and turned and strode down the mountain.

Charlie was sitting in his favorite easy chair facing the piano and grimaced ruefully when Daisy walked into the cottage. "I made an ass of myself, didn't I?"

"No, I know it's difficult for you." She closed the door and took off her shawl. "All great artists have temperament. Look at Van Gogh. He cut off his ear." She tilted her head. "Both of yours appear to be in place."

"I'd give an ear for his talent." He stretched out his legs in front of him. "Hell, I'd give an arm or a leg. Where's Jason? Did I scare him off?"

"No." She avoided looking at him as she draped the shawl over the back of the chair at the kitchen table. "We went for a walk and then he went back to his hotel."

"I was rude to him."

"He understood."

Charlie nodded slowly. "He's a complicated man, but I think he's capable of understanding a great deal." His gaze narrowed on her across the room. "He's the one, isn't he?"

She stiffened. "The one?"

"The one who will bring you the joy I knew with your mother." He smiled gently. "I'm glad he came now, Daisy. Don't be afraid to reach out and grab the brass ring just because my carousel is winding to a halt. There's nothing I want more than for you to be happy and safe."

"It's not like that." Her words came haltingly. "We're just friends, Charlie."

He shook his head. "Don't lie to yourself. You love him. Life's too short to waste even a minute of it deceiving yourself."

"No, I . . . you're wrong. I don't—" Her eyes widened in shock as the mysterious knowledge that had eluded her while Jason was looking down at her suddenly emerged bright and shining from the mist. Joy and tenderness, the desire to nurture as well as hold. Love. "How did you know?" she whispered.

Charlie smiled and got to his feet. "I always had a keen artist's eye." His smile faded. "Too bad I don't have the talent to match." He started toward his bedroom and paused at the door to look back at her. His expression was loving as he repeated softly, "Go for the brass ring, Daisy."

The next moment the bedroom door closed behind him.

Daisy turned out the light and moved jerkily toward her bedroom. How had it happened? She had never intended to fall in love with Jason Hayes. She couldn't even have named the moment wariness had eased into desire, sympathy, and admiration, nor when friendship had turned into love. Yet there had been enough clues. Why else had she turned to him tonight and asked him to make love to her? Such aggressiveness was completely out of character for her. Had Charlie's outburst been only an excuse for her to take what she wanted? Even tonight, when she had come so close to the answer, she had lied to herself.

It was no wonder she had tried to convince herself that her feelings weren't deeply involved. Heaven only knew there was no future in a relationship with Jason. He wanted two things, to have her sexually and to possess her voice for his music.

No, that wasn't true. He *liked* her.

But there were no guarantees liking would turn into love, and she would be a fool to expose herself to the lacerations of unrequited love when she was already an emotional basket case. She would be much smarter to extricate herself from any further involvement with Jason.

Go for the brass ring, Charlie had said.

But if she dared to reach too high, she might fall off the carousel entirely.

She crossed to the window and sighed wearily as she leaned her warm forehead on the cool glass pane. Her instincts had always been to be open and optimistic, to give on the chance that she might receive, but the pain and waiting had gone on too long. She didn't know if she could lower her defenses and risk any more hurt. Sweet heaven, she just didn't know what was best any longer.

Four

"Hi, Charlie." Jason walked into the cottage the next afternoon without knocking, as he usually did these days, his gaze immediately going to the platform where Daisy sat posing in the big throne chair. He nodded politely. "Daisy."

She felt the color rush to her cheeks and her hand clutched her shawl closer. This was the man who had made wild love to her and now he was behaving as if they had merely exchanged handshakes. Well, what had she expected? It had been her first experience, and what had happened had undoubtedly meant more to her than to him. "Hello, Jason."

He looked away from her and moved toward the kitchenette. "Coffee?"

Charlie glanced absently at him. "Not now."

"I'll make it anyway and have it ready." He grinned. "I'm turning into nothing but a kitchen drudge. And doing industrial damage to these hands my piano teacher said would shake the musical world."

"The world is pretty hard to shake," Charlie said, his gaze on the canvas. "You'll get there." He paused before adding awkwardly, "Sorry I blew up last night."

"No problem." Jason plugged in the coffee-maker. "We're all entitled to an explosion now and then." He came around the kitchen bar and settled cross-legged in his favorite spot on the floor in front of the platform. "Right, Daisy?"

The explosion of which he was speaking had been purely sensual in nature. She looked straight before her and moistened her lips with her tongue. "I've already told Charlie I understood."

She was acutely conscious of Jason's intent gaze on her. Her pulse accelerated as she remembered his words from last night about his fantasies as he watched her pose. She had a sudden mental picture of the two of them naked in this massive Spanish chair, Jason's hands on her breasts, his hips moving . . .

Her gaze shifted helplessly, irresistibly, to Jason and then she wished she had continued to avoid his eyes. His face was faintly flushed and his expression blatantly sensual as he met her gaze. She knew he was remembering how it felt to be inside her; she knew he understood that she couldn't bear this urgent tingling between her thighs.

"Move your head a little to the left, Daisy," Charlie requested.

She jerked her glance from Jason's face and tilted her head obediently to the left. Dear heaven, she wished Jason would go away. She could feel her breasts swell against her bodice and heat flow through her.

As if in answer to her silent plea, she heard a

rustle of sound as Jason rose to his feet. But instead of leaving, he strolled over to the piano, seated himself, and began to play softly.

The haunting melody silvered through the room, the notes weaving unforgettable patterns of beauty in the air.

Daisy's hand clutched the shawl tighter around her, her gaze fixed on Jason's dark head bent over the keyboard. She was jarred from desire to a higher emotional plane that was no less powerful in intensity. Her throat tightened as she felt the tears rise to her eyes. Beautiful. Dear heaven, his music was beautiful.

Even Charlie had been drawn from his absorption. "I like that. I don't think I've ever heard it."

"I'm not surprised." Jason's eyes met Daisy's across the room. "It's from a new Broadway musical. There's no cast album out yet."

"What's it called?"

" 'Last Love,' " Jason said. "The lead soprano sings it." Jason smiled at Daisy as he continued to play. "I think you'd like the lyrics too."

She gazed at him helplessly as the music possessed her.

"Pretty," Charlie muttered, lost again in his painting.

Not pretty. Mesmerizing, heart-stopping, ravishing, Daisy thought.

"Do you like it?" Jason asked her softly.

He knew damn well she loved it. "Yes." She tried to keep her voice steady.

"Perhaps I could find the sheet music for you." She didn't answer.

"Would you like that?"

"No. I have my hands full doing Fantine."

"Well, if you change your mind, tell me." He

turned back to the keyboard. "I'm always willing to oblige."

As Lucifer was ready to oblige Eve with the apple of knowledge, she thought bitterly.

Jason continued to play softly for the next hour. He didn't confine himself to "Last Love" but he always came back to it.

Finally, Daisy couldn't take it any longer. She forced a smile as she jumped up and stepped down from the platform. "Sorry, Charlie, I have to leave early today and get this mop of a mane trimmed." She turned to Jason. "You needn't wait. I'll drive myself."

"I wouldn't think of it." Jason didn't look up from the keyboard as his fingers moved over the keys. "I don't have anything else to do."

Daisy gave him a tormented glance before she strode toward the bedroom and closed the door. As she hurriedly changed clothes, "Last Love" drifted to her from the other room.

She exploded as soon as they were out of Charlie's earshot and were walking toward the car. "That wasn't fair."

He opened the passenger door of the car for her. "You didn't enjoy the entertainment?"

"You—it wasn't fair, dammit."

"I know." His lips tightened. "But you gave me no choice. I could see from the minute I walked into the cottage today that you were pushing me away."

She waited until he had gotten into the driver's seat and started the engine before she said, "You're right. I meant to tell you that I know I made a mistake last night. I was upset and—"

"You want to go back to being buddies," he finished for her. He shook his head. "No way."

"It's best." She looked straight ahead. "I can't handle this right now."

"Then you shouldn't have started it."

"I realize it's principally my fault." She was trying to speak slowly and reasonably. "But I've thought it over and decided we can't go on with it."

His gaze narrowed on her face. "I'm not going to argue with you."

"There's nothing to argue about. My decision is made."

"Decisions are made to be changed." He started the car and edged away from the curb as he said gruffly, "I can't let you take this away from me, Daisy. Not after I had a taste of what it could be."

That was an odd way of phrasing it. "What do you mean?"

"I mean that you've just declared war." His lips tightened grimly. "And that I take no prisoners." He drew a deep breath. "Look, I don't want it to be this way. I'll make a deal with you. I'll forget about Desdemona for a while, but I've got to have something. I know damn well I can please you. Come to my hotel room after the play and let me show you."

She didn't answer.

"Will you think about it?"

She nodded her head jerkily. She would agree to anything to end this scene that was growing more painful by the moment. "I'll think about it."

After the first act that night Jason knocked perfunctorily before opening the door of the dressing room.

Daisy tensed and whirled on her stool to face

him. "I didn't expect to see you. Were you out front?"

He shook his head. "I told you I wouldn't watch you onstage again."

If she hadn't been so nervous, she would have noticed immediately that he wasn't dressed for the theater. In his fitted jeans and white chambray shirt he looked tough, male, and so sensual she felt her resolve falter as she looked at him. It's only chemistry, she told herself desperately. She had no choice about love—but lust was completely apart. If she was determined, she could fight it.

But, dear God, the chemistry was strong.

She turned back to the mirror and straightened the short curly blond wig on her head. The image in the mirror wasn't reassuring. In the loose, high-necked white cotton nightgown she had worn for her last scene she had an air of childlike vulnerability. "That's right. I forgot. Though I've never understood why you feel—" She broke off as she heard the lock on the door being turned. Her spine went rigid as she looked at Jason's reflection in the mirror. "I suppose you have a reason for doing that?"

"A very good reason. I didn't want to be disturbed." He walked toward her. "Did you intend to come to my hotel tonight?"

"I don't—" She stopped and wearily shook her head. "No."

"I didn't think so. You were definitely wobbling this afternoon." He stopped behind her, and his gaze met her own in the mirror. "Level with me. Why not? You want to come."

She moistened her lips with her tongue. "It's best that— You're a bit too ruthless for me."

"Because I upped the ante when I played *Night Song* this afternoon? That has nothing to do with this." He squatted beside her padded stool. "It's on an entirely different plane." His warm lips feathered the nape of her neck. "I hate this wig. Take it off and let me see your hair."

A hot shiver went through her and she felt suddenly weak. "It's too much trouble. It's pinned on and—" She inhaled sharply as his hands slid around to cup her breasts through the loose white cotton of her nightgown. "No," she said. "The play . . ."

"You don't appear again until the last scene. Not for almost an hour." His fingers quickly undid the bodice and slipped inside to touch her breasts. She arched forward at the shock of hard warmth of his palms against the softness of her flesh. "Plenty of time." His fingers plucked gently on her nipples, and she bit her lower lip to keep from crying out as fire streaked through her. "We weren't on the mountain last night for more than forty minutes." One hand left her and began to take out the pins holding her wig in place while the other continued to squeeze and play with her. "We could use that couch . . ."

"No, I told you—" She stopped as his warm tongue entered her ear. Another erotic shock. Why wasn't she fighting him? She felt butter-soft, pliable in his hands.

He pulled the wig from her head, and her long hair tumbled down. "Ah, that's better." He lifted a long silky strand and rubbed it slowly back and forth against his lips. "So soft . . ."

Somehow that gesture was even more erotic than the simultaneous caressing of her naked breast with his other hand. A surge of heat exploded inside her, and she sank back against him with a half-audible cry. She sat there, trembling, unable to move as he slowly rubbed her hair between his thumb and forefinger, his hand hidden in her bodice, his gaze never leaving her own in the mirror. He whispered, "Look at your face. You want this." He parted the material of her bodice so that she could see the shameless swollen, distended evidence of his words in the mirror. "Aren't you beautiful?"

She closed her eyes, but she could still hear his words.

"But not here," he whispered. "We don't want to use that couch over there. I want a bed and time to savor you. Can't you see how unreasonable you're being?"

"I can see that you're trying to hypnotize me." And succeeding, she thought, feeling utterly desperate again.

He chuckled. "It's called seduction." His smile faded. "Though hypnotism doesn't sound bad at the moment. I admit I'd like to mesmerize you into doing anything I want." His lips brushed her nape again. "Everything and anything. Would you like me to tell you how I'd start?"

Her eyes opened languidly, but she still didn't move. "No."

"Why are you so uptight?" His lips were gently tugging on a tendril of hair at her nape. "It was your choice. You initiated and I responded."

But that was before she realized how much she loved him, how helpless she was to resist him. "I'm not initiating any longer, I told you—"

"It was a mistake." As he finished the sentence his lips tightened grimly. "Too late. You had your chance to back out last night. Maybe it would have been better for both of us if you had. But now we have to play it out until the end."

She laughed shakily. "That sounds like a threat. I know you wouldn't use force, Jason."

"No, but anything else. I'm feeling wild." He stood up, his hand still lingering in her hair. "I won't give up, Daisy. If you don't come to me tonight, I'll be here tomorrow. I'm afraid I've learned to reach out and grab what I want." He smiled crookedly. "Before it's taken away from me."

Grab the brass ring.

He reached into his pocket and pulled out a hotel key and placed it on the vanity. "I'll be waiting."

She stared blindly down at the metal key as he moved toward the door.

"There's nothing to be afraid of, Daisy." He paused at the door. "You'll have nothing but pleasure with me. Will you come?"

She didn't answer, and a moment later the door closed behind him.

Dear heaven, her body ached with need and she was shaking uncontrollably. She couldn't take this. She leaned forward and buried her hot face in her hands. She knew now Jason would never give up until she gave in to him. Just pretending everything was all right, getting through every day with Charlie, was a battle now, and she couldn't endure more conflict on another front. What did it matter if she got hurt? At least she could seize a little happiness and forgetfulness now.

Grab the brass ring.

* * *

Jason lay propped against the headboard of the bed with only a sheet covering his naked hips when Daisy let herself into his hotel room.

The room was dark except for the lamp burning on the bedside table, and she hoped he couldn't see how tense she was. She felt vulnerable enough without a spotlight revealing her nervousness.

Jason's tense muscles visibly relaxed when he saw her in the doorway. "You took a hell of a long time."

"I wasn't sure I was coming at all. I can't stay long. I have to get home to Charlie." She moistened her lips with her tongue. "You have to understand. Charlie comes first. A few hours after the performance won't matter too much, but that's all."

"Oh, I understand." He smiled crookedly. "Now that I'm properly warned of my unimportance in the scheme of things, do you suppose you could come in and shut the door?"

She closed the door and drew a deep, tremulous breath. "I feel very strange. I've never done anything like this before."

"Then I'd better convince you that it's worth your while to stay." He threw aside the sheet and got out of bed. She caught a glimpse of strong thighs, massive chest, rampant arousal as he snatched up a midnight-blue robe from the chair by the bed and strode toward her. He took her purse and tossed it on the chest beside the door and handed her the robe. "Bathroom." He patted her matter-of-factly on the derriere and pushed her toward a door leading off the bedroom. "A hot shower to relax you and you'll be fine."

She looked at him uncertainly and he grinned reassuringly and winked at her.

How odd to have a naked man wink at you, she thought, bemused, as she moved toward the bathroom. After the spellbinding seduction to which she had been subjected in her dressing room, Jason's lightness put her off balance. She disappeared into the bathroom and turned on the shower.

Jason was wrong; the shower did little to relax her. She was too conscious of him waiting naked just beyond the door. After she had dried herself she slipped on the dark blue velour robe, took off her shower cap, and let her hair flow down her back. She reached up and tentatively touched a lock brushing her shoulders. Her breasts swelled against the soft material of the robe as she recalled Jason rubbing those strands back and forth across his lips. Her heart was suddenly slamming against her rib cage. She had been half joking about him hypnotizing her, but she couldn't deny the physical magnetism he held for her. Sweet heaven, she wanted him.

She took a deep breath, turned, and opened the door. He was sitting on the chair across the room, one leg thrown over the arm of the chair as natural and at ease as if he were fully clothed. She wished desperately she could be as calm.

His gaze searched her face and his eyes widened. "I'll be damned, I think you're afraid of me."

"No," she said. "Yes." Her hand fumbled nervously at the belt at her waist. "I told you I wasn't used to this kind of thing."

He rose slowly to his feet and came toward her. "I should have had you under me in that bed two minutes after you walked into the room. Then you wouldn't have had time to think about—" He stopped before her and reached out his index finger to gently touch her left cheek. "I wanted to show you how patient and gentlemanly I could be. Hoisted on my own petard." His hand fell away from her cheek and he stepped back. "Well, I'll have to repair my fences, won't I?"

"What do you mean?" She watched in bewilderment as he crossed the room, lifted the heavy easy chair in which he had been lounging, and carried it to the center of the room. "And what on earth are you doing?"

"Setting the stage. Too bad we don't have a platform." He slanted a reckless smile at her, then positioned the chair beneath the small amber and crystal chandelier in the center of the bedroom. "You're going to pose for me."

She blinked. "What?"

"You heard me." He pushed her gently back into the big chair before going over to the wall beside the door and turning on the overhead light. "I want to make damn sure you want me as much as I want you." He came back toward her. "As much as you wanted me this afternoon in the cottage when you were posing for your father." His fingers brushed her throat and a shiver went through her. "But you weren't really posing for Charlie, were you? It was for me. You were remembering I told you last night how I fantasized about you when you posed. When you looked at me, I knew you were wondering if I was still thinking about the two of us in the chair." He settled himself on the floor a few yards away and crossed his legs as he had that afternoon in the cottage. "And we both know I was." He smiled coaxingly. "Pose for me, Daisy."

The hot color stained her cheeks. "I . . . can't. I feel foolish."

"But excited?"

She was surprised to find her nervousness ebbing, submerged by the sheer erotic strangeness of the situation. "Yes," she whispered.

"Do you want to know what I'm thinking now?"

Her fascinated gaze met his across the room. His face was taut, his light green eyes shimmering, his lips heavily sensual.

"Yes."

"I'm thinking how fair your hair looks against the dark blue of the robe." His voice lowered. "And I'm thinking how much I'd like you to take the robe off. Will you do that for me, Daisy?"

His tone was coaxing, but again she had the feeling of being mesmerized by the sheer force of his will. "Do it," he repeated softly. "I didn't get the chance to savor you last night. I want to look at you."

Her fingers began automatically to fumble with the belt at her waist while his words flowed over her. "That dark texture makes you look as fragile as Venetian glass. Your skin glows against it, and your hair . . ." His gaze wandered down to her bare feet peeping out from underneath the hem of the robe. "It's funny how bare feet can make you look completely vulnerable."

The sash was untied, but she hesitated, shy, uncertain.

"Take it off," he said thickly, still staring at her feet.

She took a deep breath and slipped her arms from the robe and let it fall to the cushions of the chair in back of her.

Jason's gaze moved with excruciating slowness up her ankles to her calves to her thighs, lingering for a moment on the curls that encircled her womanhood before traveling over her belly to her breasts. "What an exquisite surprise. The rest of you is so delicate and fine-boned and then to see that beautiful fullness . . ." He smiled as he saw her nipples begin to harden beneath his gaze. "Tell me what you're thinking."

"I feel like a slave girl sitting before a sultan," she said shakily.

"That's not reasonable when you're on the throne and I'm the one at your feet." His gaze lifted to her face. "You're only giving me my fantasy and posing for me."

She wasn't sure anymore whose fantasy this was. She felt excitement building higher and higher within her with every passing moment. Dear heaven, his eyes . . .

"Kneel on the chair." His voice was hoarse. "And bring your hair over your shoulders to cover your breasts."

She moved dreamily, languidly, to obey him.

"That's right. Now, just stay there and let me look at you."

The atmosphere in the room was thick, charged, electric. She found her breasts lifting and falling beneath the veil of her hair as she struggled to force air into her constricted lungs. The moments stretched on. He didn't move.

"You're trembling," he said raggedly.

She was doing more than trembling. She was shaking like a leaf in a storm. She could do nothing but stare at him, at the smooth, powerful muscles of his shoulders, bunched, ready, and yet leashed. At the brawny thighs dusted with fine hair, at his chest with its dark triangle . . .

"But so am I."

He was suddenly on his feet, moving across the

room toward her. With one movement he scooped her up, swiveled, and dropped into the chair. "It's time. I can't stand it any longer." He fitted her to him and sank into her with one plunge and then was still. His chest was moving heavily, frantically, as he buried his face in her hair. "Lord, I didn't think I'd make it." His hands gripped her hips, sealing her to him. "Hang on, it's going to be a wild ride."

He began to move, thrusting, bucking upward.

It was wild, and hard and nearly animalistic in its intensity—and exactly what Daisy wanted. The eroticism that had gone on before had whipped her responses into a frenzy and she heard herself moaning, gasping, as they moved closer and closer toward climax.

When the release came, it was as wild and explosive as the journey itself, and Daisy could only cling desperately to Jason while ripple after ripple of sensation washed over her.

She collapsed against him, her hair flowing over his chest, her breath coming in short, sobbing gasps.

She was so dazed, she was scarcely aware of Jason's gentle hand stroking her hair. "You see," he said huskily. "We have to have this." His lips brushed her temple. "No matter for how short a time. We have to have it."

Passion, not love. No strings . . . A bittersweet sadness rippled through her.

His lips moved to caress her ear. "You'll come again?"

Passion wasn't enough, but at this moment she couldn't afford to throw it away. Whatever he could give, she needed so she could get through the days ahead. "I will."

His hand stroking her hair stopped in mid-motion. "Every night?"

How could she stay away? The bond between them was growing stronger, tauter, with every encounter. She buried her face in the dark, springy hair thatching his chest. "Every night."

"What are you doing?" Daisy raised herself on one elbow, her eyes straining in the darkness to see Jason's naked silhouette framed against the moonlight pouring through the window across the room. "Don't you feel well? Is something wrong?"

"No." His shoulders moved as if throwing off a burden. "Just thinking. I'm sorry I woke you."

"I didn't mean to doze off. I have to go soon." She sat up in bed and brushed her tangle of golden hair back from her face. He wasn't telling the truth. In that instant of waking she had sensed a sadness, a poignant loneliness. "Thinking about what?"

"You." He gestured with his hand to encompass their situation. "This. We're very special together, you know."

Hope leapt within her. "Are we?" It was the first indication that he had even given any thought to their affair. Conversation had been low on their list of priorities during these past two weeks that had been an erotic dream. During the time they spent with Charlie at the cottage Jason maintained the same casual, friendly cheerfulness, but she was always aware of an underlying tension in him. He could scarcely wait for her to walk through the door of his hotel room before joining with her, and then the only words between them had been feverish mutterings of lust and frantic need. They couldn't get enough of each other, and she had been as frantic as he in their couplings. She seemed to want him all the time now. Color stung her cheeks as she remembered how she had made him pull over to the side of the road the night before on the way home to the cottage. Her eagerness had made him wild, and he had driven into her with— She blocked the thought and said dryly, "I don't know about special, but we're enthusiastic anyway."

"No, it's more than that." He was silent, looking out into the darkness at the street below before he said haltingly, "It's like a song."

She wrapped the sheet around her and sat back on the bed. "A song?"

He nodded. "That's how a song usually comes to me. Out of the darkness, completely unexpected, and yet suddenly it's there." He turned and walked toward her. "Playing over and over in my head until I have to put it on paper and let it out before it will go away." He stood over her and reached out to cup her face in his unsteady hands. He whispered, "*You're* like a song. I have to play you over and over."

"So that I'll go away?"

"No." His fingers tangled in her hair as it usually did, and he pulled her head back to look down into her eyes. "No matter how many times I play you, you don't go away." His head bent, and he kissed her with exquisite gentleness. "I start hearing you again as soon as I've finished."

Her throat tightened with tears, and to keep them from falling she had to make a joke of it. "Daisy's theme?"

He nodded. "It's as good a name for it as any."

He pushed her back on the bed. "Daisy's theme." He parted her thighs and moved between them. "Gentle and shining and honest. I lay beside you and I hear it. You leave me and I still hear it." His hands searched and found her. "But you're here now and the cresendo's building."

"Jason, I have to go. I've been here too—" She stopped as his fingers sank deep, probed, and began a lazy rhythm. She gasped and her spine arched up off the bed toward him.

"Soon," he muttered. "I don't want to let you go. One more time. I have to play you again. . . ."

"Stay the night."

Daisy looked over her shoulder at Jason lying naked on the bed as she slipped on her blouse. She felt a hot shiver ripple through her as her gaze ran over him. He was all brawny muscle and arrogant male power. They had made love twice tonight, and yet she suddenly wanted him again. "You know I can't do that. I have to get home."

"Just a quickie and then home to Papa?" He saw the hurt clouding her expression and muttered a curse. "I'm sorry." He threw the covers aside and jumped out of bed. "I'll be with you in a minute."

She slipped her foot into her low-heeled sandal. "Perhaps I'd better take my own car from now on. It makes no sense for you to have to get out of bed every night to take me back—"

"I said I was sorry," he interrupted roughly as he disappeared into the bathroom. "I know you never stay. It just came out." She heard the sound of running water in the basin.

She put on her other sandal and sat down on

the bed to wait for him, a troubled frown knitting her brow. Jason had been moody as the devil since two nights before, when she had awakened to find him standing at the window. Not surly, just tense, and at times she thought she could detect an element of desperation. "I know it's inconvenient for you to—"

"Crap." He came back into the bedroom and began dressing. "I don't mind the drive." He tucked his shirt into his pants and slid his feet into his moccasins. "I guess it's the Othello in me."

She looked at him, puzzled.

"I'm jealous." He picked up his jacket from the chair where he had tossed it and smiled sardonically as he shrugged into it. "I once told you that you had that crazy, effect on me."

"Jealous of Charlie?"

"I don't have a bigger rival." He picked up his wallet and keys from the table and jammed them in his pockets. "Or one who's harder to fight." He crossed the room and pulled her to her feet. "Come on, let's go."

She stared at him, puzzled as she moved toward the door. "But you like Charlie."

"That why he's harder to fight." His hand tightened on her elbow. "Does he know about us?"

"Yes." She glanced at him soberly. "But not from anything I've said. He's not blind or stupid. Before, I posed for him after the performance every night."

One corner of his lips rose in a lopsided smile that held a touch of bitterness. "And I guess I'm pretty obvious to Charlie. I can't look at you these days without getting hard."

His bluntness surprised her. "I'm the one who's

obvious. Charlie's always been able to read me."
Her hand clutched nervously at her bag. "I've
never wanted to deceive him."

"He wants the best for you." With suppressed
violence he punched the button for the elevator.
"I know damn well he'd relocate to New York if
you starred in *Night Song*."

She didn't answer.

"And you know it too. Why the hell won't you—"

"He's lived here for the last fifteen years. He's
happy here."

"And what about you?"

"I'm happy too. I don't need *Night Song*."

"But you want it," he said softly. "I saw it on
your face when I was playing 'Last Love.'"

"It was beautiful. I'm a singer and naturally—"

"You want it."

She met his gaze steadily. "Yes, but I'm not
going to take what I want. Forget it, Jason."

"The hell I will." The elevator doors slid open
and he stepped into the cubicle. "Lord, you drive
me crazy. You look like the most gentle angel this
side of heaven and you have the obstinacy of a
mule."

"I'm being perfectly reasonable."

"Reasonable people don't throw away chances
like *Night Song*."

"Please. I don't want to talk about it anymore."

He glanced at her strained expression and
relented. "Okay, we'll forget it for now." His
mouth tightened. "But I'm not giving up."

She knew he wouldn't give up anything he
wanted. She had discovered his will was as impla-
cable as it was irresistible. She sighed resignedly.
"I know you won't, Jason."

Five

"Would you like to come in and say hello to Charlie?" Daisy asked as she reached for the handle of the car door.

"I might as well." Jason got out of the car and came around to stand beside her on the street. "I haven't seen him since yesterday." He slanted her a look shimmering with recklessness as he started up the walk toward the cottage. "Maybe I'll play him another number from *Night Song*."

"No!"

He stared at her with mock innocence. "Whyever not? He liked it." He added softly, "And so did you."

"I thought we weren't going to talk about this." She glanced sidewise to see the same dark moodiness she had noticed before in his expression and asked quietly, "Why do you want to hurt me?"

"I don't want to hurt you." He shrugged wearily. "Or maybe I do. Tit for tat."

"I'm not hurting you."

"Aren't you? Then why does it feel as if you

are?" He threw open the door and stepped aside to let her precede him. "Never mind. It's a moot question when I—"

"Charlie!"

Charlie was lying sprawled in his favorite easy chair, one hand hanging limply over the arm. His face in the half darkness was as still as marble.

"Oh, dear God!" Daisy pushed past Jason, raced across the room, and fell to her knees beside the chair. She could feel something warm and moist running down her cheeks. "No, Charlie!"

"Daisy . . ." Charlie muttered as he opened his eyes.

Relief poured through her, and she collapsed back on her heels. "You were only asleep." She ran a shaking hand through her hair and laughed tremulously. "You're such a workaholic, I never expected to see you sit down on the job. Lord, you scared me."

"Did I?" Charlie reached out and touched her wet cheek. "I got disgusted with that stupid fruit and gave it up."

"It's not stupid." She smiled brilliantly at him. "But I'm home now. Wait until I change and you can work on the portrait."

"That's good." His blue eyes twinkled. "Your skin tone's much more of a challenge than that idiotic banana's." He looked over her shoulder to grin at Jason. "Stay and watch, Jason? We'll put you to work running us coffee to keep us awake."

Jason's arrested gaze was still fastened on Daisy. He forced himself to look at Charlie and shook his head. "I refuse to be used as an errand boy at two in the morning. I just dropped in to say hello. I'll run along now." He lifted his hand in farewell. "Maybe I'll come by to chew the fat tomorrow evening while Daisy's performing, Charlie."

"Do that." Charlie wrinkled his nose. "Anything's better than facing that awful banana."

"Thanks," Jason said dryly as he moved toward the door. "I'll pick you up at three tomorrow, Daisy. Good night."

"Good night." Daisy scarcely heard him. She was already heading for her bedroom to change, her entire being filled with profound thankfulness.

Not yet. It wasn't going to happen yet.

"What's wrong with him?" Jason asked as soon as Daisy got into the car the following afternoon.

Daisy stiffened. "I beg your pardon?"

"You heard me. Stop treating me as if I were feebleminded." Jason put the Mercedes in gear and pulled away from the curb. "Last night it would have been clear to anyone that Charlie was asleep, but it threw you into a panic."

"I made a mistake," she said evasively. "Charlie never falls asleep that early and I—"

"Bull," Jason said succinctly. "Everything fell into place last night. I should have suspected something before now, but he doesn't look sick."

"I didn't say he—" She broke off as he glanced directly at her. It was no use trying to fool him any longer. "All right, he's sick."

"How bad?"

"It couldn't get much worse." She didn't look at him. "It's a blood disease that generates blood clots. Very rare." She paused. "And fatal. He's had it for over five years and it's getting worse. He's already had one heart attack. The doctor said the next one would kill him."

"Are you sure? There are discoveries made every day."

She smiled sadly. "I'm sure. Do you think we didn't explore every possibility? It's too rare a disease to merit any all-out effort to find a cure."

"How long does he have?"

"It could happen anytime. A few weeks, a month. A year at the outside. So you can see how impossible it would be for me even to think of leaving."

His hands gripped the steering wheel. "May I ask why you didn't tell me?"

"I promised Charlie. He didn't want anyone to know. He wants to live a totally normal life until the end."

"So you let me try to bulldoze you, harass you, and didn't say a word. Do you know how that makes me feel?"

"I promised Charlie," she repeated. "I keep my promises, Jason."

He was silent for a moment. "Yes, you do, don't you?"

"And you can see why I can't play Desdemona?"

"Yes." His foot jammed on the accelerator. "I can see why you can't leave him."

She glanced at him, puzzled. His grim expression chilled her, and she said haltingly, "I'm sorry I couldn't tell you. I know you must feel you've wasted a great deal of time trying to talk me into playing Desdemona."

"Don't be ridiculous. I don't feel like that at all."

"What do you feel?"

"Sad for you and Charlie. Frustrated that I can't wave a wand and make it all right."

Relief surged through her. He wasn't angry.

"Stop looking like that." His tone was ragged.

"Did you think I'd be bastard enough to think about myself and my damn play while you're going through this?"

"I didn't know what—the play's so important to you."

"So are you."

She went still. "Am I?"

"Too damned important." He drew up before the theater and leaned across to open the passenger door. "I'll see you tonight."

She nodded, her eyes shining radiantly as she jumped out of the car. He had said she was important to him. There was the faintest possibility he meant he loved her. "Tonight."

She slammed the door and walked quickly into the theater.

"She knows," Eric said as soon as Jason picked up the phone. "God, I'm sorry. I warned him. I thought for sure Jessup wouldn't—"

"When?" Jason asked curtly. "When did Jessup tell her?"

"Last night."

"Then she could be on her way now."

"Not yet. I bribed the desk clerk at Claridge's to call me when she checks out. You'll have warning."

"Thanks, Eric."

"I got Bartlin for Iago."

"What? Oh, that's great."

"What about Justine?"

"No, she can't do it."

"Rats." Eric's voice brightened. "But if you already know that, maybe Cynthia's timing isn't so bad for once. She won't interfere with your negotiations."

"No, she won't do that."

"Jason?" Eric hesitated. "What's wrong. You sound . . . funny."

"Do I? I wonder why?"

"Look, if you need more time, maybe I could stall her. I can go see her and—"

"No! Stay away from her." Jason made an effort and steadied his voice. "It will be all right. I just have some details to wind up here. Let me know when she checks out of the hotel."

"Okay." Eric paused. "What will you do then? Come to London?"

"No, I'll take a plane to New York, tie up a few details, and then go to Eaglesmount."

"Back into your hermit's cave?" Eric asked sourly. "Can we count on you to come out for the opening?"

"We'll see. When you find a decent Desdemona, let me know and I'll check her out." But he knew there would never be a Desdemona like Daisy. "Look, I have to go. I have some things to do."

"Right. I'll be in touch."

Jason hung up the phone and closed his eyes as wave after wave of despair and pain washed over him. Lord, he didn't want it to end. Dammit, it couldn't have happened at a worse time. Why couldn't he have had a few more weeks before the curtain fell? Daisy was going to need him and he wouldn't be there.

The tigers have never come to me.

Well, the tigers were drawing closer to Daisy every moment, and he wouldn't be around to protect her or to help heal the wounds.

Not if he was to save her from the most ferocious tiger of all.

He dropped down on the chair beside the desk

and tried to clear his mind of pain and anger. He couldn't have what he wanted, but at least on this occasion he had a little time to try to help where he could, to ease the way for the people he had come to care about.

"So stop feeling sorry for yourself," he muttered. "Get off your duff and get to it."

He reached for the telephone on the desk. First, he would call the manager of the theater, and then go to the cottage and see Charlie.

He couldn't keep the tigers from coming, but maybe he could add salve to ease some of the pain from the wounds they would inflict.

"Hi, Charlie! Got time to stop for a cup of coffee?" Jason strode into the cottage and moved toward the kitchenette. "I know, don't tell me. Make it myself. You're too busy."

"Don't you ever work?" Charlie looked up from his easel. "You don't seemed worried about making that part-time job steady."

"Actually, I got a telephone call when I got back to town tonight. I have to go back to New York for a while, so I dug up a replacement for a few weeks."

"Bad news?"

"Depends on how you look at it." Jason plugged the coffeemaker into the socket. "Nothing I can't handle."

"There's not much of anything you can't handle, is there, Jason?"

"I have my problems like everybody else." Jason strolled out of the kitchenette toward the easel. "What are you working on?"

"Daisy's portrait. I should finish it tonight."

"Are you going to show it to her?"

Charlie shook his head. "Not yet. I'm saving it."

"For what?"

"I want her to know how I feel about her after—" Charlie stopped, was silent a moment, and then turned to look at Jason. "She told you, didn't she?"

Jason shook his head. "I guessed it and she affirmed. She'd never break a promise to you." He paused. "I hope you don't mind."

"I don't mind. You've practically become family." Charlie's gaze shifted back to the portrait. "You'll take care of her?"

"I promise she'll have everything she's ever wanted."

"That's good." Charlie moved his shoulders as if shrugging off a heavy burden. "I was worried about her before you came along. She's too loving for her own good, but you're tough enough to keep her from harm."

"Yes, I'm tough enough." Jason swallowed to ease the sudden tightness of his throat and looked hurriedly back at the painting. "It's good, Charlie."

"It's the best thing I've ever done. It's no masterpiece, though," Charlie made a face. "I guess I wasn't destined to be immortal."

"Is that what you want?"

Charlie nodded. "I suppose it's basic instinct to want to create something beautiful to live on after you."

"But you've already done that."

Charlie looked at him in surprise.

Jason nodded toward the painting. "Daisy."

"I told you I didn't—"

"Not the painting. I don't have the knowledge

to tell whether the portrait is special. I was talking about Daisy herself. There's no question Daisy is a very special creation."

Charlie's expression softened. "No question at all, but she's not my creation. I'm only her stepfather. I didn't give her that voice."

"God gave her the voice," Jason said quietly. "But you made sure it was trained. You guided her and formed her values. She *shines*. And you polished her and gave her that radiance."

Charlie shook his head.

"Listen to me, it's true." Jason's voice vibrated with sincerity. "You've created something much more enduring than a painting. Everyone Daisy comes in contact with feels a little better, warmer. Every time she sings, she gives gifts, and you're the one who gave us that." He clapped him on the shoulder. "Isn't that almost as good as being Rembrandt, if not better?"

"No." Charlie's eyes were twinkling. "But it comes pretty close. Being Svengali ain't so bad."

"Being Svengali is pretty damn good." Jason turned and went back to the kitchenette. "Now, I'll give you that cup of coffee and you can get back to work. You know, I've been thinking. I know a few people in New York art circles who might want to take a look at the portrait. We may be able to get you a shot at immortality after all. Will you let me borrow the picture for a few weeks and give it a try?"

"To put my mind at ease?"

Jason shook his head. "I'm no do-gooder. It just occurred to me that you weren't looking at your accomplishments in the right light. You're one of the most successful men I know." He glanced back over his shoulder. "And a damn fine human being."

Charlie nodded his head in acknowledgment as he followed Jason to the breakfast bar. "I return the compliment. Daisy has excellent taste."

Jason poured coffee into two mugs. "Daisy gives everyone the benefit of the doubt. She can't tell the gold from the dross."

"You think you're dross?"

Jason handed the mug to Charlie. "With a few golden moments."

Charlie gazed at him thoughtfully. "I believe you may be wrong."

Jason shrugged. "Well, I'm right about Daisy and I'm right about you too, Charlie." He lifted his mug in a mock toast. "To Daisy."

Charlie lifted his own cup and a gentle smile lit his face. "To Daisy."

Jason collapsed on top of her, his chest heaving, his entire body shaking.

Daisy's own breath was coming in gasps, and it took a few moments to steady it before she asked, "Is something wrong?"

She could feel Jason's muscles harden against her. "Why do you ask that? Did I hurt you?"

"No." He had been careful not to hurt her, but the tempo of their lovemaking had been wilder than ever before, almost brutal in intensity, and she had sensed great desperation in Jason's possession. "No, but I—" She stopped as she felt Jason's lips tugging at her earlobe and his unmistakable arousal pushing against her thigh.

"Again?" she whispered. "So soon?"

"Again. He parted her legs and moved over her.

With one stroke he filled her to the hilt. "And again." He drew out and began plunging wildly. "And again."

Jason was definitely acting very strangely tonight, Daisy thought uneasily. He had showered with her, helped her to dress, and now was leaning against the jamb of the doorway of the bathroom, watching her as she stood before the mirror combing her hair as if he couldn't bear to have her out of his sight. She glanced at him with a worried frown. "Jason, are you sure that—"

"I love your hair," he said thickly. "Lord, it's beautiful."

He loved her hair. He loved her body. She felt a jab of pain at the knowledge that he always spoke of the physical, never the total person. "I should really cut it. It tangles terribly."

"No!" She looked at him in surprise, and he smiled with an effort and said less violently, "You must do as you think best, of course, but it would be a mistake." He glanced away from her. "I'll always remember how your hair looked spilling over that pillow."

Her hand stopped in midair as a chill swept through her. "Remember?"

"I have to get back to New York."

She quickly lowered her lashes to veil her eyes. "You do?"

He nodded jerkily, still not looking at her. *"Night Song."*

"Will you be coming back?"

"It's not likely."

"Of course." She put the comb down very carefully on the marble vanity. "I understand. There's

really no reason you should stay here now that
you know I can't play Desdemona."

"It's not—" He broke off, and for an instant she
thought she saw a flicker of torment on his face.
She must have been mistaken, for the next
moment his expression was impassive. "I have to
leave Geneva."

"How soon?"

"This morning. I have a flight at six A.M. I'll
throw my suitcases in the car and drive directly
to the airport after I drop you off at the cottage."

She mustn't let him see the pain flowing through
her. She should have expected this. He had been
honest with her. He had told her his music was
everything to him. "You don't have to take me
home. I can take a taxi."

Jason's lips tightened. "I'm taking you."

"I think I'd rather you wouldn't." She tried to
keep her voice steady. "I seem to be having a few
problems maintaining control. I'm not really good
at saying good-bye."

"Daisy, I don't want—" He broke off and then
said hoarsely, "I'm sorry it had to be this way."

"Am I making the situation difficult for you?"
Her lips stretched in a frozen smile. "I have no
claim on you. You've never made me any promises."
She pushed past him, grabbed her jacket from
the chair, and headed for the door leading to the
hall. "Good-bye, Jason. Good luck with *Night
Song*."

"To hell with *Night Song*." He reached her in
three strides and whirled her to face him. "Dammit, I can't *help* it."

"You have your priorities." Her voice was brittle, but at least it was no longer shaking. "I told
you I didn't blame you, but you know I'm not very

sophisticated. I can't seem to handle this in the approved, civilized fashion." She was struggling to get away from his touch. It was incredible that even through the pain engulfing her, she still wanted him to touch her, hold her. "Just let me go. I have to get home to Charlie." She broke away and turned toward the door, her words tumbling out feverishly. "He'll miss you. Why don't you drop him a postcard from New York?"

"I've already said good-bye to Charlie."

"Have you? That's good." She jerked open the door. "I really have to go." She was half running down the corridor toward the elevator as she spoke. "Charlie . . ."

"Daisy!"

She paid no attention, and a moment later the elevator doors closed behind her and the elevator started to make its smooth descent to the lobby. She mustn't cry. If she wept, her eyes would be red and puffy and Charlie would know. Charlie had enough to face without having to comfort her. After all, she had understood this would happen sometime. No strings, he had said. She was stupid to think Jason might learn to feel the same love for her that she felt for him.

Oh, Lord, it hurt!

But she mustn't cry. Charlie mustn't know.

She paused on the doorstep of the cottage and took a deep shaky breath, trying to form a game plan.

She wouldn't be able to fool Charlie into believing she didn't care that Jason had gone, but she could pretend all was well between them and Jason had gone away for only a short time. Then she'd have an excuse for being upset but not heartbroken. Yes, that would be the best course.

She swallowed, pasted a bright smile on her face, and went into the cottage. The room was lit by the lamp on the table by the door, leaving only shadows beyond the pool of light. She had been so upset she hadn't noticed that the house wasn't flooded with the brilliant light Charlie required to work.

"Charlie? I guess Jason told you that—" She broke off, an awful feeling of déjà-vu sweeping over her.

Yes, that was it. It wasn't real. This was just a memory of that other night, when she had made the terrible mistake.

But it was real.

Charlie wasn't asleep in the armchair, he lay crumpled on the floor in front of the easel.

"Charlie?" she whimpered. "Oh, God, no."

And the tigers come at night. . . .

Daisy hadn't expected there to be so many people at the funeral. She hadn't realized how many friends Charlie had in the colony. Artists were basically solitary folk, and there was little socializing among them. Yet here they were, sober, awkward, a little uneasy, to say a last farewell to Charlie. She blinked the tears from her eyes as she turned away from the grave.

"I wonder if I could speak to you a moment, Miss Justine?"

Daisy turned to see Eric Hayes standing beside her. Jason's brother, not Jason himself, she thought with a sudden jolt of pain followed immediately by a violent wave of anger. She didn't want

Eric here with his polite murmurings of sympathy. She had gone through enough in these past few days without being reminded of both her naïveté and the hurt she had suffered because of it. "What a surprise to see you," she said coolly. "I'm afraid I don't really feel like conversation, Mr. Hayes."

"Eric." A flush reddened his pleasant features, and for an instant she felt a flicker of remorse. It wasn't Eric's fault that the sight of him brought back all the pain of her last evening with Jason.

"I know this is lousy timing," Eric muttered. "And I wouldn't have bothered you, but I promised Jason."

"I beg your pardon?"

"Jason sent me to help you. He couldn't come himself."

Of course he couldn't come to Charlie's funeral. He was busy with *Night Song*. Besides, he would be appalled if she misunderstood sympathy for something deeper. She accepted both those facts, but it didn't keep her from feeling a smoldering resentment toward him. He may have crossed her off his A list, but, dammit, Charlie had been his friend and he should have been there to say good-bye. "I don't need help."

"Please." Eric put his hand on her arm. "Jason doesn't often ask favors of me. I'd appreciate it if you'd let me give him what he wants."

"I don't see—" She broke off as she saw his pleading expression. Why not? It didn't make any difference. "All right, we can talk while you walk me to my car."

Eric breathed a sigh of relief and fell into step with her. "Now, what can I do for you? I'm sorry you had to make all the funeral arrangements by yourself. The manager of the theater didn't notify Jason of your father's death until day before yesterday.

Her eyes widened. "Why would he notify Jason?"

"Jason called him before he left Geneva and asked him to let him know if you—" He paused before adding awkwardly, "Experienced any problems."

"I see. How kind." She tried to keep the bitterness from her tone. Jason was a possessive man, and she supposed it wasn't beyond the realm of possibility that he could feel a certain responsibility toward her after taking her virginity. Perhaps, in his own way, he was even genuinely sorry about Charlie's death. "I'm sorry you had to go to all this trouble. Before Charlie died I didn't know how I was going to survive it. But I have." She met his gaze. "I found out that if you reach down deep enough, you can handle almost anything. I don't need any help."

"Look, why don't you use me?" he asked coaxingly. "I'm great at handling insurance companies and movers and stuff. I even enjoy it."

"Movers?"

"Well, you won't want to live in that cottage any longer." He added matter-of-factly, "Memories are hell." He hesitated. "Besides, we kinda hoped you'd come to New York now."

Stunned, she turned to look at him.

"Desdemona. There's really no reason why you can't take the role now," Eric said. "You'd be crazy not to do it. It will send your career soaring."

"I'm afraid you've come for nothing. I still don't want to be in your brother's play."

Eric was silent a moment. "It's Jason, isn't it?

He told me you might resent him." He appeared faintly embarrassed as he continued. "I don't know what's between the two of you, and it's none of my business. I'm just playing messenger boy. So let me do my job. Okay?"

His boyishness was appealing, and she found herself softening toward him. "I'm sorry, none of this is your fault. What's the message?"

"He said to tell you that if you take Desdemona, you won't see him until opening night unless there's an emergency." He grimaced. "Maybe not even then. He's been known to miss his openings on occasion."

She gazed at him uncertainly. "He wouldn't be in New York?"

Eric shook his head. "He never leaves his estate in Connecticut unless there's a glitch in the works."

"That seems odd."

"It's crap," Eric said flatly. He gestured impatiently. "But that's beside the point. Jason would be out of your hair."

Pain flashed briefly within her and then faded into a dull ache. "I don't know."

"Jason said you liked the music."

"What I heard of it."

"It's all super." Eric smiled coaxingly. "I know Jason can be difficult, but why give up a job that can put you up there where you belong just to spite him? Jason keeps his promises."

"I know he does."

"Then what's the hold-up? I'd say it's the medicine you need under the circumstances." They had reached the car and he opened the driver's door for her. "You should keep busy." He grinned.

"And I've hired a director who'll guarantee to work the socks off you."

Work. The concept filled her with longing. To be able to work so hard she'd fall into bed at night and not lie awake thinking of either Jason or Charlie. Not only work but the gift of that enchanting, mesmerizing music.

"You're tempted." Eric sounded gleeful. "Why not give yourself what you want, what you need?"

She got into the car and sat there gazing at the wrought iron gates of the cemetery. "Because I'm not sure what I need right now."

"I'll drop by later this evening." He frowned in concern. "Will you be okay? My wife, Peg, is back at the hotel. Should I bring her with me?"

She shook her head. "No strangers. I'm not up to it."

"Peg's not a stranger." He grinned. "When you meet her, you'll understand." His smile faded. "But I'll come alone. Eight?"

"If you like," she said wearily. Lord knows she didn't want to be alone tonight. It was going to be difficult enough going through Charlie's possessions and deciding what she wanted to keep and what to give away. "Eight o'clock."

She found the note in the middle drawer of the desk.

Just a careless scrawl that she instantly recognized as Charlie's lying on top of a stack of bills and receipts. She supposed it was a will of sorts. Charlie had never wanted to think of death, and it came as a shock that he had made this attempt at setting matters straight.

AN UNEXPECTED SONG • 101

To my daughter, Daisy, I leave all my love and possessions with the exception of her portrait, which I leave to my friend, Jason Link—who is less dross and more gold than he thinks.

Shock upon shock. He must have written this note sometime during those last days, perhaps even that very last day.

She slowly stood up and moved toward the covered painting on the easel. She hadn't been able to bear touching any of Charlie's paintings since his death. So much love and effort had gone into them that they were far more intimate than any clothing or other things.

She took off the drape cloth and looked at the portrait.

She stood there a long time, gazing at the canvas with tear-bright eyes as afternoon faded into dusk.

Love. Jason had said the portrait was filled with love and he had spoken truly. She knew she would never be able to look at this painting without remembering Charlie and their life together. This was a legacy far more precious than the worldly goods Charlie had mentioned in that pitiful scrap of a note.

The note. This painting belonged to Jason! Dammit, she didn't want to give it up.

And she didn't actually have to give it up, she thought fiercely. Surely that note wasn't legal. Even the name in the bequest was wrong. If Charlie had known what the circumstances were, he would have—

How did she know what Charlie would have

done? She slowly put the drape cloth back on the painting and wearily turned away. She knew she couldn't ignore Charlie's last wishes. The painting would have to be packed up and shipped to Jason.

She glanced around the room and pain surged through her. She couldn't stay here. There were too many memories and this part of her life was over forever. She had to move on. Why not make the move that would give her the most satisfaction? Jason had not let his feelings stand in the way of his music, so why should she? She wasn't that same soft, quivering bird caught in the eagle's spell any longer. She had met the tigers, endured their bites, and survived. She was tough enough to face Jason calmly even if she did run into him in New York.

Grab the brass ring.

The phrase Charlie had used came back to her. He hadn't been speaking of her work but of love and commitment. Well, love had vanished but she still had her singing and there was more than one brass ring to capture in this world.

She moved quickly across the room to the phone on the desk.

"Daisy Justine just called to say she'd sign for Desdemona," Eric said as soon as Jason answered his phone. "We leave for New York day after tomorrow."

"That's good."

"Good? I thought you'd be happy as a lark."

"How is she?"

"Shaken. Hurting."

Jason's hand tightened on the receiver. Lord, he wanted to be with her. "Get her out of the cottage."

"Peg and I are going over to help her pack tonight." Eric paused. "She's changed from the first time I saw her. She's stronger than I thought, and she's showing a hell of a lot of guts."

"Stay with her. Keep her busy. Don't give her a chance to think."

"We will." Eric paused. "I don't suppose you'd like to tell me what's between you two?"

"No."

"I didn't think so. I like her, Jason. She's . . . she's special."

"Yes."

"You're certainly forthcoming," Eric said caustically. "What a way with words. Remember the critic who said that if Shakespeare was a song writer, he'd be Jason Hayes?"

"Take care of her, Eric."

Eric's tone softened. "I will. You just take care of yourself."

He hung up the phone.

Jason replaced the receiver and stood looking down at the phone. Giving Daisy the role was a risk, but only a minor one. He had exited the scene before he could be linked to her, and he would force himself to stay away from the rehearsals. Pain washed over him as he thought of never seeing Daisy onstage singing his words, never seeing Daisy again. . . .

But he had promised Charlie she would have everything she wanted and he knew this was the only way he could give it to her that she would accept.

In the meantime, thank God he had work to do. Work was forgetfulness. Work was salvation.

He turned, left his study, and went across the hall to the music room.

Six

"It's not working," Joel Rickert said flatly as he strode up the steps onto the stage. "Dammit, Daisy, what's wrong with you? I heard you played Fantine for two years, yet you do this scene as if you've never died before."

Daisy heard Eric's chuckle from his seat in the fourth row, but she wasn't amused. She was too tired and discouraged and she knew the director was right. She was botching the scene that was the climax of the play, and she couldn't seem to do anything about it.

"Fantine's death scene was different. Her death was—" She broke off in self-disgust as she realized she was about to make a lame excuse. How unprofessional could she be? "You're right, Joel. I stink in this scene."

"Well put." Joel Rickert grudgingly turned to Kevin Billings, who played Othello. "You're doing a decent job, Kevin." He shot a sour glance at Daisy. "He almost makes you look good."

Daisy flinched. "I'll try to do it better."

"*Try?*" Joel asked caustically. "Two weeks until opening night and you're going to try? Don't you think it's time you did more than try?"

"Take it easy, Joel," Kevin said soothingly. "It'll come. She's terrific in the rest of the play."

"Keep out of this, Kevin." Joel turned on him. "And don't be so damned stupid. If she blows this scene, she blows the entire play."

Daisy felt a flicker of irritation toward Joel as she saw the flush that reddened the skin above Kevin's beard. Kevin had only been trying to help, and Joel didn't have to take his frustration out on him. In the past six weeks of rehearsals she had grown very fond of Kevin Billings. Though he had the acting range, powerful physique, and magnificent voice required for the role of Othello, offstage she had found him to be as friendly and unassuming as a puppy with none of the annoying ego usually displayed by stars of stage and screen. "Leave him alone, Joel. Don't attack Kevin when I'm the one at fault."

"You're damn right you're at fault," Joel said grimly. "And if you'd put a little emotion into this scene, I wouldn't have to attack anyone." He threw up his hands. "Do you think I like being the bad guy?"

Maybe he didn't like being the heavy, but he was utterly ruthless when he felt it was necessary. But that was part of good directing, and Joel Rickert was a very good director. "I don't know why I'm having trouble with it. I'll work on it."

"Yes, you will." Joel's lips tightened grimly as he turned on his heel and ran down the steps to his seat in the fourth row, where Eric Hayes sat watching. "And you'll get it if we have to stay here all night."

He meant it. Daisy had learned in the past six weeks of rehearsals that Joel always meant exactly what he said. If she didn't perform to his satisfaction, they'd be doing this scene until they all dropped from exhaustion.

Kevin's hand squeezed her shoulder comfortingly. "You'll get it next time."

She forced a smile. "You say that every time I blow it. You must have the patience of an angel."

"It's worth a little patience when I know we're creating something special," Kevin said gravely. "The music . . . you and me . . . don't you feel it?"

She did feel it. That's why she had put up with Joel's ranting and raving and his frenetic pace. *Night Song* had all the elements of being a blockbuster that might run for a decade. However, what was more important was the dual challenge of creating an unforgettable character and serving the music. "Yes, I feel it. *Night Song* is special." She smiled at him. "And you're right, it's worth all the hassle."

He nodded. "What do you say we go out and eat chili after we get through this? I know a great place, and a good meal always relaxes me."

"Sure, why not?" She made a face. "If we ever do get through this."

"Again,' Joel said. "From the top."

Daisy took a last swallow of the hot tea she'd requested to soothe her throat, and gave the empty cup back to the stagehand. Dear heaven, she was tired. "Can't you send the rest of the cast home? It's almost midnight and they—"

"How can I do that?" Joel interrupted caustically. "You obviously need all the help you can get."

"It's all right," Kevin whispered to her. "I don't mind. You'll get it this time."

Daisy smiled wanly. "I feel like Eliza Doolittle in *My Fair Lady*."

"I've always wanted to play Henry Higgins." He struck a pose and clowned. "By George, she's got it." His smile faded as he studied her pale face. "And you'll get it too."

She smiled at him. "You'll be a much better Othello than Henry Higgins."

The pianist began to play "Last Love."

Poor man, she thought, the pianist must be as tired as the rest of them. Wearily, she moved toward the stripped-down bed that was the only prop in the center of the stage. She knelt on the bed and listened for her intro.

"Wait!"

She went rigid and stared straight ahead at the first button on Kevin's shirt. Oh, no, she didn't need this now.

Kevin's gaze searched the darkness of the auditorium. "Who the hell is that?"

"Jason," Daisy wasn't even aware she had whispered the name. "It's Jason."

"Hayes?" Kevin asked with interest, squinting as he tried to make out the shadowy figure coming down the aisle. "I've never met him. He's something of a recluse, isn't he?"

"Yes." Her lips felt dry, and she moistened them with her tongue. She had told herself she would feel nothing when she saw Jason Hayes again, that what had happened between them had been due to her vulnerable state preceding Charlie's death. Yet the moment she had heard him speak she had started to tremble. "So I've heard."

"You recognized his voice. You know the great mystery man?"

"I've met him." She forced herself to look over her shoulder to see Jason stop at the row where Eric and Joel were sitting. Her glance raked over him as he began speaking to Joel in a low tone. He was dressed in black jeans and a long-sleeved black shirt that made his big, muscular body look more slender than she remembered, but the guarded expression was the same and so was the impact of that riveting presence. "But I don't think I ever really knew him."

"His music is fantastic." Kevin frowned: "Lord, what if he doesn't like the way I'm playing Othello?"

Even easygoing Kevin was a little intimidated. "What's not to like? You're wonderful." She spoke without thinking, her gaze still on Jason. "I'm the problem child."

But she wasn't a child any longer, certainly not the naive child who had fallen under Jason's spell all those weeks before. Dear heaven, she prayed she wasn't still that child.

"Are you okay?" Kevin asked gently, his gaze on her face.

She forced herself to look away from Jason and smiled with an effort. "Evidently, Eric called the great man and told him I was endangering his precious play."

"You think so?"

"What else would bring him here at midnight?" She stood up, consciously bracing herself. "He's come to the rescue."

"Well, he can't be any tougher than Joel."

"Don't bet on it." She had received a firsthand

lesson on how ruthlessly singleminded Jason could be where his music was concerned. Well, she had enough of waiting like a victim while her executioners discussed which ax to use. She took a step toward the apron of the stage and called down into the darkness. "Hello, Jason. I must have been pretty bad if they had to call you in as a reinforcement."

Jason turned to look at her, and she inhaled sharply as she received the full force of that blue-green gaze. "Rotten," he said tersely. "I've been watching you for the last hour from the back of the theater, and I couldn't believe it."

Maybe she had gotten over him, she thought desperately. There had been a time when she had been so acutely conscious of his presence that he couldn't have walked into a room without her sensing his arrival. "You're not going to get an argument from me."

"I don't want an argument. I want a performance." He smiled grimly. "And I'm going to get it." He turned to Joel. "I think I've located the problem. Cut the lights and clear everyone from the stage."

"You heard the man." Joel motioned to the light technician in the booth and the theater was suddenly in darkness.

"A spotlight on Desdemona," Jason called.

"My name is Daisy," she said with a touch of defiance as she was pinned in a circle of stark light.

"Wrong. Right now you're Desdemona. Get in the wings, Billings."

Kevin frowned uncertainly. "Wouldn't it be better if I stay and help? I can give her something to react to and—"

"No, it wouldn't," Jason interrupted curtly. "You're part of the problem."

Daisy bristled. "The devil he is. No one could be more supportive than Kevin. It's not fair to blame him for my lousy performance."

"Get into the wings," Jason said to Kevin as he started up the steps to the stage. "Let's get this over with."

Kevin shrugged and the next moment faded away in the darkness, leaving Daisy alone on the stage with Jason.

"Kneel on the bed," Jason said. "You're waiting for your lover."

Pose for me. Kneel on the chair.

No, that time had nothing to do with the present.

She knelt on the bed and nodded for the pianist to start the music.

"No accompaniment," Jason said swiftly. "You don't need it. You know the music. It's a part of you, part of Desdemona."

She looked at him, startled.

He stepped into the spotlight and she immediately became aware of their isolation from the watching cast and crew in the wings. "He's your lover but you fear him. You know he suspects you of being unfaithful, and he's a violent, tormented man. You've undressed and put on your nightgown." He stepped closer and reached out and slowly began to take the pins from the chignon in which her hair was bound and dropped them one by one on the bed in a gesture of excruciating intimacy.

She mustn't remember how many times he had done that before, how many times he had draped her hair over her naked breasts or stroked his body with its softness. Dear heaven, she *was* remembering, she realized helplessly. The air seemed to thicken, become charged, and her breasts were swelling against the cotton of her blouse.

He combed her hair with his fingers until it flowed about her shoulders. "You've taken down your hair. You've been careful to say your prayers because you know you may not live until the morning."

"Is all this necessary?" she asked shakily.

"Yes, the mood is everything. That's what's wrong with the scene." He looked down at her, his light eyes shimmering in his dark face. His voice lowered to a whisper. "Billings is a good actor, but he's not giving you what you need."

He arranged her hair over her breasts as he had so many times before. Only then he had leaned down and put his rough cheek against them and rubbed back and forth until she had moaned and pulled his— She blocked the thought, but it was too late. Her heart had already begun to slam against her rib cage. "And what do I need?"

"Fear. Uncertainty." Jason's lips tightened grimly. "You're clearly bosom buddies with Billings. You know he'd never hurt you, and it shows in your performance. Desdemona loved Othello, but she also feared him. She was all light to Othello's darkness. You need to *feel* the fear so you can draw on it when you need it."

She raised her brows with a touch of mockery. "And you're going to furnish me with the necessary darkness?"

"Oh, yes." He smiled bitterly. "I've always been Othello to you, Daisy."

Her eyes widened as she realized he spoke the

truth. Even in their lightest moments together she had been aware of a darkness, an element of danger in him that had made their relationships more exciting even as it had intimidated her.

He nodded slowly as he read her expression. "You didn't realize that? I always did." He stepped out of the spotlight into the darkness. "From the very beginning. Sing 'Last Love,' Daisy."

He was only a dark, massive silhouette in the shadows beyond the spotlight, waiting.

She experienced a sudden flutter of panic.

The demand came again, soft, seductive, irresistible. "Sing for me, Daisy."

She began to sing, her voice at first shaking and quavering in the darkness. Then suddenly the stage disappeared, everything faded away, and she became the gentle, doomed Desdemona. Othello, her lover, was there waiting, watching her, brooding, intense. So much violence. So much hurt. She wanted to reach out and soothe him, take away the pain, but she was too frightened. Couldn't he see she'd never be unfaithful to him? Couldn't he see how much she loved him?

He moved, shifted, and she caught the glint of his light eyes glittering pantherlike in the darkness. She caught her breath. Now? Was he going to strangle her now? She could barely force the last line of the song through her lips as she gazed at that beloved, menacing shadow standing in the darkness.

The last line of the song silvered in the night like a frantic heartbeat about to be stilled as she waited for him to come to her. She lowered her head in silent acceptance of her fate.

Applause.

She didn't need the spontaneous applause from

the cast in the wings to make her realize she had made the transition. For those brief moments she had truly been Desdemona.

She dazedly lifted her head as Jason stepped into the spotlight again, his lips twisting in a crooked smile. "I really do scare the hell out of you, don't I?"

"No." She straightened and looked him directly in the eye. "Othello scares Desdemona. You don't scare Daisy."

A flicker of surprise crossed his face and then he nodded slowly. "I see that I don't. Eric said you'd changed." He paused. "But you'll always remember how Desdemona felt whenever you sing that song, won't you?"

"Yes." She searched and found the pins he had dropped from her hair and hastily fastened it up again. "I will remember. Thank you for that." She stood up and faced him. "Though I know you did it for your play, not for me."

"Did I?" He smiled curiously. "How well you know me." His expression turned bleak. "But perhaps not well enough. I'm not all Othello."

"All right, that's fine, Daisy." Joel strode toward them from the wings. "Now let's try it one more time with Kevin."

"No." Jason turned away and moved toward the wings. "She's exhausted. Send her home, Joel."

Joel frowned. "Look, what if she can't do it again? We've got to hone it and develop the nuances and—"

"She'll be okay. Send her home."

"By George, she's got it." Kevin grinned as he bounced toward her. "I told you that you'd do it." He picked her up and swung her in an exuberant circle. "Now can we have chili?"

Jason stopped and turned to look at them. His face was expressionless, but she suddenly had the same feeling she had known when he had stood passionate, possessive, menacing in the threatening darkness.

She shifted her shoulders uneasily and then lifted her chin with a touch of defiance. She was Daisy, not Desdemona. If she was to build a new life without him, she had to learn to ignore the dark fascination he held for her.

She deliberately turned away from Jason and smiled brightly at Kevin. "Definitely chili. I'm starved. Give me twenty minutes to shower and change and I'll meet you at the stage door."

Daisy's pace faltered as she came down the dimly lit corridor.

Jason was leaning against the wall beside the stage door and a faint smile touched his lips as he saw that slight hesitation. "Right on time. Don't worry, Billings didn't stand you up. I sent him out into the alley to wait for you."

"Why did you do that?" Her stride quickened briskly as she moved down the hall toward him. "I thought you'd gone."

"No." He straightened away from the wall. "I wanted to speak to you."

"Did you?" She smiled brightly. "Some other psychological insight into Desdemona? You needn't have bothered. The last scene was the only one I was having trouble with."

"I know. Eric says you're going to be fantastic in the role."

"How nice."

"How are you getting along? Eric told me he'd

found an apartment for you in Greenwich Village. Are you comfortable?"

"Yes, Eric and Peg have been very kind to me."

"You're easy to be kind to."

"Really?" She met his gaze. "You didn't seem to find it easy."

He stiffened. "I was as kind as I could be under the circumstances."

"The hell you were. You once accused me of using you, but I believe you take that prize. I was a babe in arms compared to you." She held up her hand as he started to speak. "Oh, you gave me fair warning. In fact, at first I blamed myself for being foolish enough not to heed you." She gazed at him directly. "But then I realized you knew I wouldn't pay any attention to warnings, Jason. You *knew* me. You're such a clever man, and you knew it was perfectly safe to take anything you wanted and still feel self-righteous about it."

"I hope I was never self-righteous."

"But you admit you knew I wasn't in your league."

He smiled faintly. "On the contrary, you were way out of my league."

She shook her head. "I was clay in your hands. You mesmerized me."

"You're speaking in the past tense." His voice was mocking. "Are you telling me you've recovered from my so-called Rasputin maneuvers?"

She nodded. "I woke up when Charlie died."

His smile disappeared. "I wanted to be with you, but I—"

"Don't lie." Her voice was shaking, and she tried to steady it. "If you'd wanted to be there, you would have come. You knew what you did to me that night, and then to come home and find Charlie—" She had to stop as that memory rushed back to her. "I was bleeding inside and you let me face it alone." She stared at him defiantly. "Well, I faced it and I learned from it."

"That I'm a bastard?"

"No," she said quietly. "That I was a fool to think you could really care about me."

He looked as if she had struck him. "You weren't a fool."

She felt the tears stinging her eyes, but she refused to let them fall. "A blind fool." She blinked back the tears and smiled bitterly at him. "I didn't even realize you were one of the tigers, Jason."

"I'm not, dammit." His lips twisted as if in pain. "I've always wanted to help you."

"Oh, yes, you want to make me a star." She shrugged. "Well, you're doing that, aren't you? And you're getting what you want at the same time. Clever, Jason." She swallowed hard to rid her voice of huskiness. "However, I'm glad you waited. I wanted to talk to you."

"I think you've said enough. I'm still writhing under the lash."

"Did you receive the portrait I sent you?"

He stiffened warily. "Yes."

"I want to buy it back from you."

"It's not for sale."

Her hands clenched into fists at her sides. "Charlie's will probably wasn't even legal. I didn't have to send the picture to you."

"But you're a woman of honor, and Charlie wanted me to have it."

She gestured impatiently. "It was an impulse. He scarcely knew you. I know he wanted me to have that portrait."

"I think he had a reason for giving it to me."

She laughed shakily. "He gave it to you because he thought I was in love with you. Wasn't that silly?"

"Very silly." His voice was hoarse. "But you still can't have the portrait. I have plans for it."

"Dammit, it *means* something to me."

"It meant something to Charlie too."

"This isn't easy for me." She closed her eyes and whispered, "Please. Let me buy it from you. It's all I have of him."

"Daisy, don't you know I want—" He broke off and then said. "I can't do it."

Her lids flicked open and she gazed at him with eyes glittering with tears. "Dear heaven, you're cruel."

His face was pale as he nodded slowly. "Yes."

She made a low sound as she started past him. "Now that we've established that fact, you'll have to excuse me. Kevin is waiting and I—"

"Let him wait." His tone was suddenly fierce. "What the hell is Billings to you?"

"Anything I want him to be." She opened the stage door. "And none of your business."

"That's what I told myself." He grasped her elbow to help her down the step to the concrete landing.

At his touch, erotic heat stroked through her. Her gaze flew to meet his.

He smiled with savage satisfaction. "You see? He'll bore you. You're too much alike. All that sweetness and light will give you indigestion."

"Maybe I like sweetness and light. There's certainly nothing wrong with it."

The fierceness in his expression was replaced by an unutterable weariness. "No, there's nothing wrong with it. It's normal and nourishing and safe. Stick to it, Daisy, and don't let anyone talk you into anything else."

His abrupt about-face caught her off guard. "Not even you?"

"Especially not me. We've already established what a self-serving bastard I am. Why should you make me an— What the hell!"

A blinding flash of light had illuminated the darkness, and brilliant dots danced before Daisy's eyes.

As she closed her eyelids tightly for an instant she heard a low, triumphant laugh and the pounding of feet on the concrete of the alley.

"Damn him!" Jason released her arm and ran down the steps and chased after the shadowy figure bolting toward the street.

"What's he in such a fit about?" Kevin strolled out of the shadows at the foot of the steps. "It's only a picture. He got a shot of me too."

A flashbulb, Daisy realized with relief. Just a fan taking pictures. "What a persevering camera bug. It's nearly one in the morning."

Kevin shrugged. "It happens all the time here. If they get a good enough shot, sometimes they can sell it to the tabloids for a nice piece of change. A photo of you and me wouldn't pull in much loot, but a picture of Hayes might bring in a bundle." Speculatively, he looked toward Jason's running figure. "He was really mad. I wouldn't like to be in that guy's shoes when Hayes catches up to him."

"He won't hurt him," Daisy said quickly.

"How do you know?" Kevin's gaze shifted back to her face. "I thought you said you didn't know him."

"I know him well enough to be sure he wouldn't hurt somebody who couldn't defend himself." Kevin was still looking at her curiously, and she hurriedly changed the subject. "Where are we going for this fabulous chili?"

"Acapulco Sam's. Do you think we should wait around and see if Hayes catches the shutterbug?"

"No, he won't expect me to wait. We'd finished our conversation."

"Good. Then chili ho." He took her arm and gently propelled her toward the street. "Guaranteed to burn your taste buds to death and send them to heaven."

"Do they have anything tamer? I've had my fill of exotic dishes."

"Have you?" Kevin's expression became arrested and his gaze returned to the place at the end of the alley where Jason had disappeared. "Then we'll have to find you something that isn't quite so stimulating, won't we?"

Seven

Twenty minutes later Jason burst into the office on the top floor of the theater, where Eric was bent going over the costume accounts. "Someone snapped a picture of Daisy and me in the alley tonight."

"Damn." Eric straightened upright in his chair. "Did you get the film?"

"I couldn't catch him. The bastard was as fast as an Olympic runner." Jason paused. "You'll have to kill the picture."

Eric shook his head. "How the hell am I supposed to do that? You don't even know what rag it's going to be sold to."

"Phone around to the different tabloids and offer double for the picture if it shows up."

"Their circulation figures are usually more important to them than our cash."

Jason threw himself in the visitor's chair beside the desk. "I have to get that picture, dammit."

"Easy. Maybe it was just an over enthusiastic fan."

"At one in the morning?"

"Well, we don't know that—"

"I can't take the chance." Jason wearily leaned his head on his hand. "I shouldn't have come. I was stupid to run the risk. How self-indulgent can a man get?"

"I'm the one who sent up the red flare."

"It's no one's fault but mine. I didn't have to listen to you. I knew the dangers. I shouldn't have come."

Eric gazed at him curiously. "Why did you? I didn't really expect you to show up here tonight no matter now much hot water we were in with the scene."

Jason didn't answer for a moment. "I couldn't stay away."

"What?"

"It was an excuse. I wanted to hear her sing my song."

Eric nodded understandingly. "The creative demon raising its pesky head."

"No." Jason got jerkily to his feet and strode toward the door. "Daisy."

"I don't understand wh—" Eric broke off, gave a low whistle, and nodded slowly. "I guess I was afraid of this. The signs were all there. I just didn't want to see them."

"No more than I." Jason's laugh held a thread of desperation. "Get that picture, Eric."

The next moment the door closed behind him.

Three days later the phone rang six times before Daisy was fully awake and another two before she managed to get out of bed and stumble to the phone on the kitchen bar across the studio apartment.

"Hello," she croaked.

"Daisy?" Eric's tone was carefully casual. "Everything okay?"

"No," Daisy muttered sleepily. "I'm definitely not okay. I'm awake when I should be asleep. I didn't get to bed until three o'clock this morning and my idiot producer is calling me on the telephone in the middle of the night."

"It's eight in the morning. I warned you Jason was a terror."

"I'm not complaining. I'm too tired to complain. What do you want, Eric?"

"When are you leaving for the theater?"

"Eleven. Why? Has Joel pushed up the rehearsal time?"

"No." Eric paused. "I've got some business in your neighborhood, and I thought I'd pick you up and drive you to the theater. I'll be there at ten forty-five."

"Okay. May I go back to sleep now?"

"Sure." Eric hesitated. "Is your door locked?"

"Eric . . ."

"Just checking. New York isn't Geneva."

"You and Peg gave me that lecture the first day I came to the big, bad city."

"It can be bad, Daisy," Eric said soberly. "Never doubt it. I'll see you soon."

Daisy hung up the phone and stumbled sluggishly back to the bed across the room. Eric's entire conversation had been puzzling and completely out of character, but she was too tired to analyze it now. She had at least one more precious hour of sleep before she had to get up and face getting ready for another exhausting day of rehearsals.

She got back into bed and pulled the covers up around her, wondering drowsily what business Eric had in this part of town.

"I thought you should see this trash." Eric tossed a newspaper carelessly onto the coffee table. "But don't pay any attention to it. It's strictly yellow journalism."

Daisy picked up the newspaper and unfolded the tabloid she had often seen on the checkout counter at the supermarket near her small apartment. Jason and her own face stared up at her from the front page. In the photograph they were gazing at each other with an identical expression that held a sensual intimacy that startled her. Dear heaven, had she actually let Jason see that look of desire and total absorption on her face? She felt suddenly stripped, naked before the world. Another shock jolted through her as she saw the headline over the picture.

Hayes and New Star Make Sweet Music Together.

"What a nauseating play on words," she said dully. "Kevin said the picture might be sold to the tabloids."

"I tried to track it down and stop it." Eric shrugged. "But no deal."

"It seems fairly innocuous." Daisy swiftly scanned the story. "At least, it doesn't claim we're sharing a cozy penthouse somewhere."

"The tabloids have been sued so often, they try to avoid blatant libel." He paused. "But they've managed to place you both in Geneva at the same time."

Daisy looked up from the newspaper. "You're really worried about this, aren't you? Will it hurt ticket sales?"

Eric shook his head. "We're already sold out for the first eight months. A little scandal will just send sales skyrocketing."

Daisy disdainfully tossed the newspaper back on the coffee table. "Then I refuse to worry about it. Joel gives me enough headaches without paying attention to this garbage."

"Very sensible," Eric said, relieved. "I just thought you'd want to know." He took her elbow and urged her toward the door. "Now we can forget about it." He didn't look at her as he opened the door. "By the way, Peg wants you to come and stay with us for a few days."

She looked at him in surprise. "Why on earth?"

"Why not? I thought you liked Peg."

"You know I do." She shook her head. "But with the way rehearsals are running, I can't commute from Long Island to Manhattan at all hours."

"Sure you can. We'll just put a limousine at your disposal." He grinned. "Every star should have a limousine."

"I'm not a star."

"You will be in two weeks." Eric closed and locked the door before handing her the key. "Live the role."

"Maybe when I have the credentials as well as the title." Daisy shook her head. "Tell Peg I appreciate the offer, but it will really be more convenient for me to stay here until the play opens."

"Daisy, I believe you should—" He broke off, his lips twisting ruefully. "I didn't think I'd be able to persuade you, but I thought I'd give it a shot." He took her elbow and started down the flight of stairs. "But with the tabloid boys on your trail, at least let me stick around and beat them off with a stick."

She looked at him in surprise. "Is this what all your concern and the invitation is about? Aren't you lending this story too much importance?"

"Maybe." He smiled easily. "But I'd feel better if you'd let me play Galahad. Guys like me don't get the chance very often."

"But I don't need . . ." She saw the disappointment on his face and smiled gently. "I'm sure Peg sees you as Galahad."

"Yeah." He nodded. "Yeah, she does." His eyes twinkled. "But then, she's a lady of rare vision, and I feel the need for a wider audience." His expression sobered. "So let me pick you up and take you home until all this hullabaloo with the press dies down. Okay?"

She hesitated and then nodded. "Okay, but it isn't really necessary, Eric."

"I think it is." He paused. "And so does Jason." He felt the muscles of her arm stiffen beneath his grasp, and he looked down at her. "He wants to help you, Daisy. Don't shut him out."

"So he sent you to fill in for him again." Her lips twisted bitterly. "Just as he did when Charlie died." She strode on ahead of him, opened the front door, and went out onto the street. "I don't have to shut him out, Eric. He does it himself."

He muttered something beneath his breath and hurried after her.

"Eric, wait!"

Daisy turned to see a dark-haired woman in a red suit hurrying along the street toward them.

Appearing to be in her middle thirties, she had wide-set dark eyes, blue-black hair worn in a sleek chignon, and an exquisite madonnalike face that was at odds with her voluptuous body. She reminded Daisy of a flamboyant hibiscus; stunning, exotic, completely dazzling.

She heard Eric utter a soft curse.

The woman stopped before them and smiled sweetly. "Eric, it's so good to see you. We never seem to run into each other anymore."

"We move in different circles."

The woman nodded sadly. "But only because you and Jason close me out." She sighed. "How I miss the old days."

"We're in a hurry, Cynthia."

"Don't be rude," the woman chided, her magnificent black eyes shifting to Daisy. "Introduce me to your friend."

"I think you know who she is."

Her eyes widened innocently. "Whatever do you mean?"

"Never mind." Eric said. "Daisy Justine, this is my stepsister, Cynthia Hayes."

Daisy's eyes widened in surprise. "How do you do?"

"Very well. I always make sure of that," Cynthia said with a brilliant smile. "I'm delighted to meet you." She wrinkled her nose. "Though I have to confess Eric was right. I did see that ghastly article in the *Journal* and had to come along and meet you."

"You shouldn't have bothered. The article was a pack of lies," Daisy said.

Cynthia's smile widened. "Oh, but the ally a kernel of truth in every lie." Her voi ered to dulcet sweetness. "And you're pretty little thing. I read that you grew up in Europe?"

"Switzerland."

"I've been skiing in St. Moritz." She paused. "I almost went to Geneva once, but I discovered it wasn't necessary."

"Come on, Daisy, we'll be late." Eric pushed Daisy toward the car at the curb. "Good-bye, Cynthia."

"I'll see you later." Cynthia stood watching them. "I wish you'd tell that tiresome man at the stage door to let me attend the rehearsals. I'd love to see this darling thing perform."

Eric stiffened. "The rehearsals are closed."

Cynthia's smile remained in place. "But then, they're always closed to me, aren't they? Jason never realizes how he hurts me when he does that."

Eric didn't answer as he hurriedly opened the passenger door for Daisy.

"It was very nice meeting you, Miss Hayes," Daisy said automatically as she got into the car.

"Cynthia. I'm sure we have far too much in common ever to be formal with each other." The brunette's smile took on added voltage. "And it's Mrs. Hayes. Didn't you know? I'm Jason's wife."

Daisy couldn't bring herself to speak until Eric had pulled away from the curb and driven over two blocks.

"He's . . . married?" She asked jerkily, looking straight ahead. How foolish to feel this hurt and betrayal when Jason and her own relationship was over.

"No," Eric said. "Not anymore. Not for a long 'me. Jason married Cynthia when he was nineteen and she was only seventeen. They were divorced two years later."

"She doesn't seem to remember that."

"Cynthia has always believed what she wants to believe."

"Then she must still care for him."

"As much as she can care about anyone."

She swallowed to ease the painful tightness of her throat. Cynthia Hayes had appeared very pleasant, but it was clear Eric had no use for her. Still, if the woman loved Jason, it was cruel to let her suffer. "Then perhaps I'd better pay her a visit to assure her that there's really nothing between Jason and me. Where does she live?"

"No!" She glanced at him in surprise at the violence in his voice, and he tempered his tone. "Jason wouldn't like you to interfere. Their relationship is . . . complicated. Stay away from her."

"All right." Lord knows she had no desire to become involved in any relationship between Jason and his ex-wife. She was still feeling too raw and bruised from the shock of meeting Cynthia Hayes—not only bruised but hotly, passionately, resentful, she realized. Jealousy. Dear heaven, she had never been jealous in her life, but she was jealous of that woman. "It was just a thought. I'll do whatever you believe is best."

Eric breathed a sigh of relief. "Good. Please avoid her. And if she asks to see you, promise me you'll turn her down."

"Why should she—"

"Just promise me. Okay?"

"If you say so. I'll be too busy for soci; ments anyway." She paused. "I don't ever seen anyone so beautiful. She's stu

"So is a blackjack," Eric said grimly. "And it's better to avoid both of them."

She did feel bludgeoned, but it would go away, she assured herself desperately. She had scarcely thought of Jason for the past two days. She would work so hard, she would have no time to think of either Jason or the beautiful hibiscuslike woman who was clearly still very much a part of his life.

Lord, she was tired.

Daisy moved quickly toward the stage door, fervently glad she had given in to Eric and didn't have to face the subway ride home. Joel had been more difficult than usual today, but she could scarcely blame him. Her concentration had been at low ebb and she deserved every scathing criticism. He'd probably be glad to be rid of her when these—

Jason.

She stopped short on the steps as she saw him standing beside the front fender of a long navy blue limousine.

"Don't argue." He straightened. "Just get in the car."

"Eric is taking me home."

"Eric *was* taking you home." He opened the passenger door. "The situation has changed. I'm not making him a target."

"A target? Aren't you overreacting? The tabloids are interested in you, not Eric."

"Please get into the car." His hands clenched at his sides. "Look, I'm not trying to kidnap you. My only object is to get you home safely." He nodded the chauffeur in the driver's seat who could only be dimly discerned through the tinted windows. "We even have a chaperon."

"I told Eric this wasn't necessary. Neither of you have to take me home."

"Either get in the car or I'll have to follow behind you." He smiled lopsidedly. "If your aim is to save time and bother for both of us, then let me take you home and get it over with."

She hesitated and then moved down the steps and across the alley toward the car. "This is ridiculous."

He opened the passenger door and followed her inside. "So is life." He slammed the door. He pressed a button and the glass between the passenger and driver section of the limousine slid down with a whoosh. "Sam Brockner, this is Daisy Justine."

The chauffeur turned his head, and for the first time she got a good look at him. He was as far from the dignified uniformed chauffeur as could be imagined. Red-haired, freckled-faced with sparkling sherry-colored eyes, he seemed little more than a teenager. The turquoise and white flowered Hawaiian shirt he wore made his hair flame even redder in contrast, and his grin lit his face with boyish warmth. "Hi, glad to meet you, Miss Justine." He started the limousine, and the car glided down the alley toward the street. "Just sit back and relax. Jason gave me your address, and I'll have you home in a jiffy."

"Thank you, Sam. It's nice meeting you too."

Jason pressed the button and the glass glided up, leaving them again in isolation. Sh___ tense, her hands folded tightly in her lap___ straight ahead.

"For Lord's sake, relax," Jason said ro___

"I am relaxed."

"You're so brittle you'd shatter into a thousand pieces if I touched you."

"I admit I'm uncomfortable with the situation." She continued to avoid looking at him. She wished he would move away. There was no physical contact between them, but he was close enough so that she could feel the heat of his body and smell the familiar heady scent of his after-shave. "But since there's no question of you touching me, there's no danger of that occurring."

"Right."

Silence fell between them, thick, charged, tingling with awareness.

She searched wildly for a way to break it. "I somehow never connected you with a chauffeur and limousine. Eric drives himself."

"Eric's temperament is better able to cope with New York cab drivers. Besides, a limousine provides me with a certain amount of privacy."

And another wall with which to surround himself.

Another strained silence.

"I met your wife today." Dear heaven, she hadn't meant to blurt that out.

"Eric told me. And she's not my wife."

"She doesn't appear to notice the distinction. She's very beautiful."

"I once thought so."

Another silence.

"Eric said you married very young." Why was she persisting in talking about the woman when every word was salt on the wound?

"Yes."

She smiled brightly. "First love is best, they say.
m sure that—"

"It wasn't love," he broke in violently. "First or otherwise."

"Sex, then. Sometimes it's difficult to tell the difference."

"Not that either." He turned to face her. "What the hell do you want me to say? I made a mistake and I paid for it. I'm still paying for it."

"It's really none of my business."

"You couldn't be more wrong. Whether either of us likes it or not, it couldn't be more your business. Lord knows I tried hard enough to keep you out of it."

Her brow wrinkled. "You're not making sense."

"I know." His expression was suddenly weary. "It doesn't matter now. All I ask is that you let me watch over you."

The heaviness in his voice pierced the wall of resentment she had built against him, touched her, moved her. "I told you once that I'm accustomed to taking care of myself."

"But you let me take care of you and didn't suffer for it."

"Didn't I?"

He flinched. "Let me put it another way. You didn't suffer from lack of care."

"I was a different person then."

He shook his head. "You just think that. Pain doesn't change us, it simply hones away all the excess baggage to reveal what we are." He met her gaze. "You're still loving and trusting and shining with life. Too loving. You give too much for your own good. Look at what you were willing to give up for Charlie. I knew the moment I met you that you'd go where angels fear to tread."

She couldn't look away from him. She h̶ odd feeling there was something importa those words, something that should mean something to her. She had a sudden memory of that moment after they had made love and she had felt close to something mysterious and cloaked in splendor.

No, this mustn't happen again, she thought desperately. She mustn't love him. She *mustn't* fall into the trap of hope again. He didn't really love her, he probably had never really loved her.

But dear heaven, there was something *there*. Something she should know. She wasn't blind, though she was beginning to think she might have been in the past. "Are you trying to tell me something?"

He opened his lips and then closed them again. He glanced away from her. "No."

Her hopes plummeted, but she persisted. "I think you are. Talk to me, Jason."

"I have nothing to say."

Walls again.

She gazed up at him in despair as the limousine drew up to the curb before her brownstone and Sam got out of the driver's seat and came around to open the passenger door.

Jason's lips twisted. "I know you've probably had enough of my company tonight. Sam will see you to your door."

"That's not nec—" She broke off and got out of the car. She was too tired and heartsore to argue with him. She turned and started across the street toward the front steps. "Good night."

"Daisy."

She stopped and looked back at him over her shoulder.

"From now on Sam will pick you up and take

you home. I won't inflict my presence on you after tonight."

She said flippantly, "I'm surprised you're not afraid the gentlemen of the press will attack him too."

"He can take care of himself. Sam was Special Services in 'Nam." Jason's gaze shifted to Sam. "Check out her apartment, please."

"Right." Sam strolled up the steps toward the front door. "No problem. She'll be fine."

Daisy shook her head. "I doubt if he's going to find anyone lurking in the hall or under my bed."

"This is New York," Jason said. "*Lurking* is the norm in certain neighborhoods."

"Not this one."

"You're getting rid of me, but you have to accept Sam. It's a tradeoff. Accept it and count your blessings."

He didn't wait for an answer but got back into the limousine and shut the door.

He was shutting himself away from her again, but no more thoroughly than he had that moment before they had arrived at the brownstone. Why couldn't she accept his words at face value? It was totally irrational for these tears to sting her eyes. She moved blindly toward the door Sam was holding open for her.

"It's going to be okay." Sam's hazel eyes shone with sympathy in his freckled face. "Honest. Everything's going to be Jake."

"Is it?" She smiled at him mistily before straightening her shoulders. "Of course it is. Come on, Sam, I'm sure you want to get this over and get home and go to bed."

"No hurry. I'm a real night owl."

"So was my father."

"Charlie? Yeah, I know. Jason told me all about him."

Her eyes widened in surprise. "He did?"

"Sure, he must have been a great guy."

"Yes, he was." She paused. "But I guess I wasn't expecting Jason to laud his praises to anyone."

He chuckled. "You're kidding me. Right? Hell, Jason wants the whole world to know what a great guy he was."

She looked him in bewilderment.

"But here I am standing around yakking instead of letting you get to bed." Sam took her elbow and propelled her toward the stairs. "Let me have five minutes for a look-see, then I'll get the hell out of here."

Eight

"The dress rehearsal went off very well tonight, I thought." Eric sat on the flower-patterned easy chair across the dressing room. "Considering everything."

Daisy grimaced as she sat on the vanity stool and slipped on flat-heeled shoes. "Considering everything that could go wrong did go wrong. Stop trying to make me feel good, Eric. It was the usual chaos before opening night and you know it."

"You don't seem worried."

She smiled serenely. "I'm not. I'm ready even if the technical crew isn't. I have a feeling that the opening tomorrow night is going to be dynamite."

"I've got the same feeling." He reached into his jacket pocket and pulled out a small envelope. "Sam stopped by while you were battling through the rehearsal and asked me to give you this."

"Why didn't he wait until he picked me up tonight?" She stood up and took the envelope. "Don't tell me he's going to let me go home

Sam's practically been my shadow since that tabloid brouhaha."

Eric shook his head. "He'll be outside waiting as usual. Has he been annoying you?"

"No, in his diamond-in-the-rough way, Sam's a real charmer."

Eric nodded. "And tough as they come." He watched her study the envelope, his gaze narrowed on her face.

The envelope was the finest cream-colored bond and the return address on the envelope was one of the most prestigious art galleries on Fifth Avenue.

Daisy carefully slit open the envelope and drew out the single engraved card.

Her eyes widened in bewilderment as she read the three lines on the invitation.

You are cordially invited to view the finest work of Charles L. Justine at eight o'clock on the evening of July 1. Black tie. RSVP.

Dazedly raising her eyes to Eric's face, Daisy said, "I don't understand. Do you know what this is all about? A showing of Charlie's work?"

"Actually only one work," Eric said quietly. "Your portrait."

She laughed shakily. "But that's crazy. No gallery would have a viewing of one picture unless the artist was Rembrandt or Van Gogh. Certainly not one by an unknown like Charlie. Why should—" She broke off and her gaze searched Eric's face. "Jason?"

Eric nodded.

"Bribery?"

"Hell no, you can't bribe a snobbish gallery like Von Krantz."

"Then how?"

Eric took a tape out of his jacket pocket and popped it into the cassette player on her dressing table. "This." He pressed a button on the recorder. "It's the first music Jason has composed outside the musical theater in over twelve years. It's being released to the TV and radio stations tomorrow together with the announcement of the exhibition. He calls it 'Charlie's Song.' "

She sat perfectly still to listen to the hauntingly beautiful music. Strength and gentleness and a triumph of love and the spirit. Charlie.

She could feel the tears running down her cheeks, but she made no motion to brush them aside. As the last strain drifted away, she continued to stare at the glittering metal of the cassette player.

Eric reached out and turned off the player. "Jason said it was a two-pronged plan. The song should generate interest in the painting, and even if the critics pan your father's work, he still has a chance of being remembered in the art world for a very long time because of the uniqueness of the presentation."

"Something to live on after him. Charlie's immortality," she murmured, blinking back more tears.

"Yeah," Eric agreed. "I guess you could call it that."

"Why didn't Jason tell me?" she asked huskily. "He did this incredibly wonderful thing and he never said a word. How can I thank him?"

"He doesn't want thanks."

Daisy jumped to her feet, snatched a tissue

from the box on the dressing table, and dabbed her wet cheeks. "Well, he's going to get it. Where is he?"

"Eaglesmount." Eric shook his head. "And he won't see you, Daisy."

"How do you know?"

"Because he gave me a message for you." He hesitated. "He said to tell you that he didn't do this for you. He wants you to know you don't owe him anything. He did it for Charlie."

"And that isn't for me? I *loved* Charlie."

And she loved Jason Hayes. The knowledge shone bright as firelight; it thundered like cymbals. Her bewilderment and hurt were gone. She didn't understand him; she might never understand him. What did any of that matter? By all that was holy, she loved him. She started for the door. "I'm going to see him."

"No!" Eric shook his head. "I tell you he won't see you." He grimaced. "And Eaglesmount has security as tight as Fort Knox. You'll never get beyond the front gate."

"Dammit." Daisy whirled to face him. "How did he expect me to react? I want to see him."

Eric smiled faintly. "I imagine he expected you to react this way. He knows you pretty well, doesn't he?"

"Better than I know him." She lifted her chin. "But that's going to change."

"He's not going to let it change."

"Why not?"

Eric hesitated.

She gestured impatiently. "Never mind. You're as close-mouthed as Jason. Tell me one thing. Does he care anything for Cynthia Hayes?"

"Good Lord, no!"

She breathed a sigh of relief. "From what he said I didn't think he did. Then it's open season."

Eric frowned. "You don't understand the situation."

"And I'm not going to understand if I'm not told. How can I understand anything if Jason won't even see me?"

"If you want to show him your gratitude, then give him a great Desdemona. This play means a great deal to him."

"Gratitude? But I want to—" She broke off and gazed at him steadily. "All right, here's the deal. Tell him I won't go to Eaglesmount if he comes to the opening." She added fiercely, "And I *don't* want him standing in the back of the theater like some two-bit phantom of the opera. I want him beside you in the fourth row, and I want him backstage after the performance to tell me how great I was. Do you understand?"

"Oh, I understand." Eric wrinkled his nose. "But I'm not sure Jason will agree."

"He'll agree if you tell him otherwise I'll be camping outside the gates of Eaglesmount. He knows I don't give up easily." She smiled tremulously. "After all, it's really his own fault. If he hadn't composed 'Charlie's sons,' I probably would never have seen beyond his Othello mask."

"Mask?"

"Never mind." She moved toward the door. "Just give him my message." She smiled brilliantly over her shoulder. "And tell him he's going to see one hell of a Desdemona tomorrow night."

*   *   *

Daisy curtsied low, her cheeks flushed scarlet with excitement while the waves of applause rocked the theater."

Kevin's hand tightened on her own, his cheeks were also flushed, his eyes shining brilliantly. "Don't look now, but I think we've just caused a happening." The jubilant murmur was audible only to her. "Lord, I feel a hundred feet tall."

Daisy was soaring too. A standing ovation, twelve curtain calls, and the audience still didn't want to let them go. She looked down at Jason in the fourth row.

He was on his feet, applauding but gazing at her with an expressionless face. Had he liked it? Had she been wrong? No, she wouldn't let herself be intimidated by his blank stare. She had let him deceive her by his wall of silence before, but she wouldn't make that mistake again.

A gamine grin lit her face, and she gave him a conspiratorial wink. She chuckled to herself when she saw his startled reaction. Then she began to move with Kevin toward the wings.

"Daisy. Daisy darling! You were wonderful!"

A familiar woman's voice issued from the first row. Peg?

Her gaze searched the audience and her smile faded.

Cynthia Hayes stood near the stage, gowned in a brilliant peacock blue, ornamented by a magnificent sapphire necklace. She was holding up a bouquet of white roses toward Daisy.

Kevin had noticed her too. "A friend of yours? I'll get them." He quickly stepped forward, reached down, and took the flowers from Cynthia with a graceful bow. He turned, gave them to Daisy, and then escorted her from the stage. "Gorgeous woman," he said. "I wonder if she likes chili."

The creamy roses in Daisy's arms were exquisite and obviously expensive, but revulsion surged through her as she looked at them. She wanted them gone. Why had the woman given them to her, she wondered uneasily. She didn't understand the gesture any more than she understood Cynthia Hayes. "I doubt it." She quickly dropped the bouquet on the prop table in the wings. "She looks more like the veal Orloff type to me."

"Don't you know her?"

"She's Jason Hayes's ex-wife."

"Oops! Then I guess you don't want these roses sitting around in your dressing room."

She glanced at him. "Why do you say that?"

"I saw the photo in the *Journal*. You're clear as water, Eliza Doolittle." He kissed her cheek. "You don't need any more flowers anyway. Your dressing room already looks like a flower garden. I noticed someone even sent you a bottle of wine."

She nodded. "Roderer Cristal. It arrived just before I went on stage. I don't know who sent it. I couldn't read the scrawl on the card."

"Then it must have been Eric. His writing could baffle the guys who deciphered the Rosetta Stone. Shall I pick you up and take you to Eric's party after I get dressed?"

"No, I'm rather tired. I think I'll rest awhile before I change. You go on without me."

"Okay." He started down the corridor toward his own dressing room, his step springy with jubilation. "Though Lord knows how you can be tired on a night like this. We're a hit!"

A faint smile touched Daisy's lips as she proceeded down the corridor to her own dressing room. She knew how he felt. And now that she had rid herself of those blasted roses, her own exhilaration and anticipation were soaring.

Jason had been in the audience tonight. He had seen and heard her make his dream a reality.

And if he had been in the audience, surely he would take the next step and come backstage.

She opened the door of her dressing room and wrinkled her nose as waves of fragrance assaulted her. Kevin was right, the scent of blossoms was overpowering and the room did resemble a flower garden. Still, a romantic rendezvous in a flower garden wasn't a bad idea at all. She had the setting, now she only needed the costume.

The costume she had chosen was a white satin gown that bared and framed her shoulders, hugged her waist and hips before cascading into rows of heavy gleaming petaled skirts like that of a flamenco dancer. The bodice revealed the curves of her upper breasts and she let her hair flow down her back with only two jeweled combs to confine it.

Costume and setting. But where was the male lead?

She drew a deep breath to try to still the butterflies in her stomach. What did she do now? All dressed up and no one to see her. Jason would come, she assured herself desperately. It hadn't taken her more than twenty minutes to dress, and the reporters had probably surrounded him directly after the performance.

She crossed to the vanity, opened the bottle of wine, and poured a little into the goblet on the tray. She needed all the warmth and bolstering she could gather. If Jason didn't—

A knock sounded at the door and she hurriedly set the goblet of wine down on the vanity. She ran across the room and threw open the door.

Jason, dark, powerful, elegant in his black and white tuxedo, stood there.

"Hello." She sounded like a breathless child, she realized with disgust. "Come in, Jason."

He didn't move. He just stood gazing at her. "You look—" He broke off, pulling his gaze away from her smooth shoulders rising from the white satin frame of the gown. "Exquisite."

"My first designer gown." She closed he door behind him. "For Eric's party. Are you going?"

"No."

"Why did I know that would be your answer?" She moved swiftly across the room toward the vanity. "Wine? It's a fantastically good year. It's one of my opening night gifts."

"No, thank you," Jason said haltingly. "I'm here, Daisy. What do you want?"

More than she was brave enough to tell him yet. "I want you to tell me I was everything you wanted in Desdemona."

"That's easy. You *were* Desdemona." He looked away from her. "I sat in that audience and you gave me gift after gift until my cup ran over. Is that all?"

"No." She cleared her throat. "But you did that very well. Here's the big one. I want you to tell me I'm everything you want in a woman."

He went still, his gaze flying back to her face. "What brought this on?"

" 'Charlie's Song.' "

"Gratitude."

"Oh, yes." A smile made her face radiant. "I'm very grateful."

"All right, now you've said it. But what I told Eric was true. I did it for Charlie, not you."

"That isn't the point. The important thing is that you did it at all." Her face glowed with eagerness. "Don't you understand? It would take an extraordinary man to go to these lengths just to give a man his dying wish. I knew that something was wrong, that I had to have misunderstood what happened between us."

"Stop looking at me like that," he said hoarsely. "And don't make me out to be some kind of saint. I did only what I wanted to do."

"But what you wanted to do was wonderful." She smiled hesitantly. "And that makes you pretty wonderful too."

"The hell it does."

She drew a deep breath and then said in a rush, "I want you to tell me you care about me."

"Of course I care about you. We once had a relationship, and it's always difficult to rid ourselves of emotional baggage when it's ov—"

"Don't do this." Daisy's hands clenched into fists at her sides. "I need you to help me."

Jason made a low sound beneath his breath and started to turn away from her. "I don't think we have any more to talk about. Can I drop you at Eric's on my way home?"

"No." She whirled and stared numbly at her reflection in the mirror. Her face looked pale and strained, and she felt beaten. She had hoped for so much more. Perhaps she had been wrong. Maybe he didn't care for her in any permanent fashion. She reached out blindly, lifted the glass of wine to her lips, and sipped it. "I don't think I'll go to the party after all."

"Of course you'll go," he said roughly. "This is your night to celebrate."

"Celebrate?" She hurled the goblet onto the floor and whirled to face him. "Why aren't you celebrating? This is your night more than mine. Why the devil are you going back to Connecticut?"

"I can't do— What the hell is wrong?"

She was swaying, she realized with panic. She was suddenly ice cold and her lungs were starved for air. "I don't feel—" She was falling. What was happening?

"Daisy!" Jason's pale face swam above her as he caught her in his arms, braced her. "What is— My God!" He wasn't looking at her but at something on the vanity—the bottle of wine. His hands closed on her shoulders as he stared down at her. "The wine. Who sent you that damn wine, Daisy?"

She couldn't answer, her throat felt frozen, the words came out in a croak. "I don't know . . . couldn't read . . . scrawl . . ."

Then she pitched forward into icy darkness.

She was cold. So cold. She huddled into a ball to try to shut out the chill.

"Shhh." Jason's low agonized voice. "Don't cry. I can't stand it. Tell me what's wrong. Tell me how to help you."

She hadn't known she was crying. She opened her eyes to see Jason's face above her. "Cold."

He immediately drew the sheet higher up around her. White sheets; stark, antiseptic cleanliness. A hospital. That's right she was ill. . . .

"Better?" Jason asked hoarsely.

Poor Jason. His eyes were glittering, his expression tormented. How she wished she could help him. He looked so alone. He was alone. Why had she never realized how terribly alone and isolated he was?

"No," she whispered. "Hold me."

His hand tenderly brushed through the thickness of her loosened hair lying on the pillow. "I shouldn't . . . You need to sleep."

She shook her head and held her arms out to him. "Hold me."

He stood up and slid onto the narrow hospital bed beside her, his arms clasping her close. Her hair was caught beneath his shoulder and his cheek was pressed against her cheek. Then, incredibly, she felt something warm and moist on her temple.

"No," she murmured, her arms tightening around him protectively. "Don't be sad. I'll take care . . . of you."

"Will you?" His voice was unsteady as his lips tightened. "I think that should be my job, love." His lips brushed her cheek. "Don't worry, just go to sleep. You're going to be fine."

She wanted to tell him she had to worry if he was in trouble. Didn't he know that was what love was all about? Perhaps he didn't know. He was so guarded and alone. In her own hurt and unrest she hadn't realized how sad he was in his loneliness.

"Stay with me," she whispered. She was too tired to help him now, but as soon as she woke up she would take care of him. . . .

"I'll stay," he said thickly. "I'll stay, love."

*   *   *

Jason was gone and Eric was sitting in the chair beside her bed when she opened her eyes again. Disappointment surged through her.

"It's okay." Eric swiftly leaned forward and clasped her hand. "Don't be afraid."

"Why should I be afraid?" Her throat felt dry and her stomach hollow. Otherwise she felt entirely well. Then a thought occurred to her and her gaze flew to his face. "Jason's all right, isn't he?"

Eric nodded. "You're the one who had to have her stomach pumped."

That's why her stomach felt so odd and her throat so sore. She reached up and rubbed her temple as the memory of those last moments before she collapsed came back to her. "The wine . . . it was bad."

"The wine was poisoned."

Daisy's gaze flew back to his face. "Poisoned!"

He nodded. "You're lucky you had only a small sip. Any more and nothing Jason could have done would have been enough."

"I don't understand." She moistened her lips with her tongue. "Kevin thought you sent me the wine."

He blinked. "Lord, no. It was Cynthia. For once she slipped up. Since you grew up in Europe, she knew you'd be knowledgeable about wines, so she had to choose one that would be sure to tempt you. That Chateau and vintage was rare enough so that the police had no trouble tracing it to her as the purchaser."

She shook her head dazedly. "Why? I don't even know her."

"Unfortunately, she considered you to be in her way. That was all that was important to her."

She looked at him blankly. "That's crazy."

"Exactly," he said simply.

"She's unbalanced?"

He nodded. "But not in any detectable way. She's what the psychology books refer to as a sociopath. She's totally without understanding or feeling for the suffering of other people. All she relates to is her own feelings." He paused. "And she has no conscience."

"You make her sound like a monster."

"Oh, she is." He smiled bitterly. "A very clever monster. The quintessential bad seed. When she began to realize she wasn't like other people, she began to study all the books on abnormal psychology to get information she could use to protect herself. She intended to do exactly as she wished and not pay the price. But to do that she had to know what was considered abnormal in a normal world. Cynthia's been given batteries of psychological tests and come out smelling like the proverbial rose. As I said, she's a very clever monster." His hand tightened on hers. "That's why we tried to protect you."

She sat up in bed, gazing at him in bewilderment as the pieces of the puzzle began to fall into place. "You've all been lying to me. You weren't afraid I'd be bothered by reporters."

"Jason didn't want to worry you. He figured you had enough on your plate with the rehearsals." He shrugged. "So we decided to protect you without your knowing it."

"You both treated me as if I were a helpless idiot." She shook her head. "Maybe I was an idiot, a blind idiot. Don't you think it's time I was told what this is all about?"

"That's why Jason asked me to come here. What do you want to know?"

"Everything," she said curtly. "Start at the beginning."

"My father married Cynthia's mother when Cynthia was sixteen—"

"Not that far back, I meant—"

"You said the beginning. That's where it started for Jason."

Jason had married the monster when he was scarcely more than a boy. What must his life have been like after making a mistake like that? "You're right. Go on."

Eric started again, "Jason was different then." His lips twisted. "You couldn't imagine the difference. He was still absorbed in his music, but he was more open, trusting. He reached out to life. He had just gotten a scholarship from Juilliard and was wild with joy." He paused. "Then Cynthia appeared on the scene. She was even more beautiful than she is now. Younger, and she appeared to be so vulnerable." His lips tightened. "And a damn good actress. She was never out of character. Always the gentle, fragile little sister. She never paid much attention to me, but she formed an attachment for Jason and followed him everywhere."

"I can't see Jason putting up with that."

"I told you he was different." He frowned. "There's something you have to understand about Jason, one of his prime drives is the desire to protect. Cynthia picked up on that right away and used it."

"He fell in love with her?"

He shook his head. "He was too much in love with his music at that time, and besides, Cynthia screwed up. She played so much on his protective side that by the time she decided she wanted to get him into bed, he thought of her as a little sister and would no more have touched her than he would have committed incest."

"But he married her."

"Because she got herself pregnant," he said bluntly. "She came to Jason crying about this creep who knocked her up and then deserted her."

"She lied?"

"No, not entirely. Cynthia always covered herself. She was pregnant all right, but Lord only knows who the father was. She convinced Jason she'd kill herself if her mother and stepfather found out she was pregnant." His lips twisted bitterly. "It was a smart move. Jason knew the mess would hurt not only her but the family, so he took steps to prevent it. He told everyone the baby was his and he eloped with Cynthia."

She murmured, "What a quixotic gesture in this day and age."

"But not unusual for Jason, not the man he was then. He worked day and night to support both of them and still keep up his studies at Juilliard. Cynthia had a little girl and named her Dana. Jason was crazy about the kid." Eric stopped. "Too crazy. Cynthia began to resent Dana."

"Her own daughter?"

"Dana was a tool that had served its purpose, and babies can be troublesome and messy." He looked down at Daisy's hand, which he was still holding. "The baby fell down the stairs and was killed when she was two."

"No." Daisy's eyes widened with shock. "You're saying . . ."

He nodded. "Cynthia appeared heartbroken and

Jason was nearly crazy with grief. No one suspected the death wasn't an accident."

"I can't believe it." Daisy felt sick. "No one would kill a helpless baby. Maybe it was an accident. She couldn't—"

"Cynthia admitted it." Eric interrupted. "A few months after the baby died, the marriage fell apart. Jason had no reason to stay and was going to leave Cynthia. She fell into a rage and told Jason she had killed the kid because she was jealous of the attention Jason gave her."

"What did he do?" Daisy whispered.

Eric's lips twisted. "As we both know, Jason isn't exactly tame natured. If she hadn't run out of the apartment, I think he would have killed her. Instead, he went to the police." His expression turned bleak. "They questioned Cynthia, but she convinced the police Jason was bitter because she was divorcing him. Then he tried to commit her to a mental institution and, after two weeks of testing, the psychiatrists turned her out with a clean bill of health."

"No!"

"She knew all the answers and the responses. She was so persuasive that by the time she left the hospital they had issued a report to the police that it was Jason who had the potential for being unbalanced and possibly had a persecution complex."

"Dear God!" Daisy exclaimed. "What did he do?"

"What could he do? He had a choice of killing Cynthia and being tried for murder or trying to get on with his life. It wasn't easy. Cynthia dogged his footsteps, begging him to go on with the marriage. No matter how harshly he rejected her, she wouldn't believe he meant it. He moved to California and tried to lose himself. She found him." He paused. "And then the accidents started."

"Accidents?"

"He had a beagle he loved. The dog ate rat poison. His secretary's car's brakes failed and she went over the cliff. She was in the hospital for over a year. His best friend had a boating accident and drowned. At first Jason thought he was some kind of jinx. Every time he grew close to someone they were either severely hurt or died a violent death. Then, gradually, he realized what was happening."

"The police."

"Accidents. I told you she was clever. Whenever he went to the police, that damn report surfaced saying he had a potential for paranoia. She cut him off, isolated him from anyone or anything he cared about. If it had been a personal attack on him, he could have dealt with it, but he couldn't risk hurt to anyone he cared about. He was afraid to let anyone close to him." He touched his chest. "Even me. Finally, he bought several hundred acres in Connecticut, built Eaglesmount, and devoted himself to his work."

"I can't believe it. He's been living in a nightmare all these years. Why didn't someone help him?" She glared at him accusingly. "Why didn't you help him?"

"I told you how protective he was. I tried to convince him I didn't care about the risk." He flushed. "But then I met Peg and the kids came and I—"

"So you let him stay in his prison. You let that woman—"

"I didn't know what else to do. I couldn't let anything happen to Peg."

"And he couldn't let anything happen to you or the rest of his world. Stalemate." She gazed at him in disbelief. "You all let her terrorize you."

His lips tightened. "May I remind you she almost killed you?"

"And what did Jason do about that?"

"He went to the police and this time they came up with a link to Cynthia. The wine." He paused. "And then he went after Cynthia. She's disappeared, but both Jason and the police are looking for her now. He said to tell you not to worry. I'm to take you home and keep you under wraps until he finds her."

"No."

"What?"

"I'm not going to hide away from that . . . that tarantula," she said flatly. "I have a show to do tonight."

"You have an understudy."

"That's *my* role."

"You're not well enough to perform tonight."

"Watch me. Desdemona was delicate anyway. It might even enhance my characterization."

"I can't let you do it. Jason would kill me if I let you expose yourself."

"Then you'll have to take your chances. It's about time someone besides Jason did." She tossed aside the cover and swung her legs to the floor. "I'm not letting Jason build me an Eaglesmount to hide away in, and I'm not going to let him continue to live like that either."

"And what are you going to do?"

"The first thing I'm going to do is to get out of here and go to the theater. I can rest there until it's time to go on. You can either help me or let me go alone."

"You're weak as a kitten."

"I'm stronger than you think."

"Yes." He studied her thoughtfully. "I believe you are."

"You'll help me?"

"Do I have a choice?" Eric asked ruefully. "I can't have you collapsing on the way to the theater."

"I won't collapse.' Her lips set determinedly. "It would give that viper a victory—and she's not going to win one more battle."

Nine

Jason was waiting in her dressing room when she finished her performance that night and jumped to his feet the moment she walked into the room. "Are you all right?"

"Other than feeling like a wrung-out dishrag, I'm fine." She strode over to the vanity and sat down. "And I don't think my performance suffered."

"I don't give a damn about your performance." His hands clamped down on her shoulders. "I couldn't believe it when Eric told me you were on stage tonight. You've made yourself into a blasted target."

"Eric said she was clever. I didn't think there was a chance she'd take pot shots at me while I was onstage. Did you find her?"

"No, but I'm still looking for—"

"Good." She began creaming the stage makeup off her face. "But I think we need to act more aggressively. If she won't let herself be found, then we'll simply have to tempt her out into the open." She looked at his reflection in the mirror. "And we're not going to do that by hiding me out on Long Island."

"Really?" Jason's hands tightened on her shoulders. "I can hardly wait for you to unveil your master plan."

"No master plan. I just intend to lead the normal life I usually lead and let her come to me."

"Bait," he said hoarsely. "I'll be damned if I let you do it. You don't know her. She'll—"

"I know she's a monster and that she's made your life hell." She met his gaze in the mirror. "And I know I'm not going to let her do it any longer. I want her behind bars, where she belongs, and I want you free."

"I've been fighting this battle since I was twenty years old. They won't jail her without hard evidence."

"We have the bottle of wine."

"Which means we have a chance. We need more evidence."

She shrugged. "Then we'll get more evidence."

"Leave this to me. She'll kill you." His face was pale. "She almost did it last night."

"Because I wasn't on my guard."

"It doesn't matter. You don't know what she is. She's like a—" He stopped, searching for a word. "I *can't* lose you."

"You don't have me." She stood up and moved toward the closet. "And you won't have me until we get rid of that python choking the life out of you."

"I'm not going to let you do this, Daisy."

"Yes, you are." She smiled lovingly at him over her shoulder as she reached for the hanger on which her tunic shirt and slacks were hanging.

"Because you can't do anything else. It's my life and I'm going to live it as I see fit."

His hands clenched slowly into fists at his sides before he turned on his heel and strode toward the door. "Not if I find her first."

"What can you do if you find her?"

'What I should have done when I learned what she had done to the baby."

"And become a murderer yourself?"

His face twisted with torment. "I won't let you die."

He slammed the door behind him.

Sam was waiting in the hall when Daisy came out of the dressing room ten minutes later. He shook his auburn head reprovingly at her. "You gulp poison one night and the next you're onstage shouting a siren call for her to come and get you again. Not smart, Daisy. You've got lots of heart, but I can't say much about your brain power."

"I suppose you've got orders to encamp outside my apartment?"

He shook his head. "*In* your apartment."

"I only have one bed."

"That's all right. I brought my sleeping bag. Jason says I stick close as glue to you from now on."

Daisy nodded. "I'm not going to argue. I have every intention of living to a ripe old age and enjoying every minute of it." She glanced at him from the corner of her eye as she started down the hall. "Do you know about Cynthia Hayes?"

"Sure, Jason told me about her when he hired me. He seemed to think she might be a threat to me if I took the job." He grinned. "But he knew I could take care of myself with that bitch."

"I'm going to get rid of her."

"It's about time."

"Will you help me?"

He nodded soberly. "Jason's my friend. You find a way to squash her and I'll provide the army boots."

She smiled. "That's good to know."

"So when do we start?"

"Not tonight. I'm still too weak and shaky." She opened the stage door. "Tomorrow after the performance will do as well."

Sam pressed the code into the panel and the electric gates slid open. "You'd better make this good. We may not get another chance. Jason's likely to have my ass in a sling for bringing you here." He drove through the gates and up the long, curving driveway of Eaglesmount.

Daisy looked up at a mellow, ivy-covered red-brick mansion that reminded her of an old English country house. She was surprised by the timeless beauty and serenity of the place. She supposed she had been thinking of Eaglesmount as a house as gloomy and melancholy as the House of Usher.

"You're sure he's at home?"

Sam nodded. "He called me at the theater while you were onstage to check to make sure everything was okay with you."

"Where will he be in the house?"

"Probably the music room. He spends most of his time there. The second door on the left when you enter the foyer." Sam drew up before the front entrance. "The code to open the front door is four-twelve-one."

"Thanks, Sam." Daisy drew her white satin cloak more closely around her as she opened the passenger door and scrambled out of the limousine. "Don't worry, everything will be fine."

"I'll go to my quarters. Call me if you need me."

He meant if Jason threw her out on her ear. But she couldn't let that happen. "I won't need you." She waved and closed the passenger door before climbing the steps and pressing the code into the panel beside the carved mahogany door.

The front door swung open and she stepped into the foyer. She was confronted, again, with beauty and timeless elegance. A graceful curving staircase swept up from a superbly designed hall in which polished black and white tiles gleamed beneath an exquisite crystal chandelier. She shouldn't have been surprised, she thought with a sympathetic pang. Cynthia Hayes had driven Jason into making this house into his haven and, because it was his nature to create beauty, he had turned Eaglesmount into an extraordinary home.

Second door on the left. She took a deep breath and moved across the gleaming black and white squares toward the music room.

Jason was sitting at the Steinway baby grand across the room, making notations on the sheet of paper in front of him. His dark hair took on added luster beneath the light of the chandelier. Dressed in gray cords and a black shirt, he seemed an anomaly in this gracious old-world house. He looked tough, sexy . . . and lonely. His loneliness sent a surge of love and sympathy through Daisy that melted her nervousness.

"What are you working on?"

He stiffened and then swiveled on the bench to face her. "What are you doing here?"

"Sam brought me." She closed the door behind

her and came toward him, her white satin cloak rustling as she walked. "Is that for a new play?"

"Yes."

She smiled. "Is there a part in it for me?"

"I don't know." He frowned. "You shouldn't be here."

"You certainly made it difficult for anyone to get to you. What security!" She stopped in the middle of the room. "But here I am and I have no intention of letting you toss me out."

He stood up and strode toward her. "I haven't found Cynthia yet. I have a detective agency trying to locate her, but you'll have to stay away from me until I—"

"The hell I will." She whirled in a circle, and the white satin cloak rippled and shimmered under the lights of the chandelier. "Isn't this a gorgeous cloak? It matches the gown I was wearing when that snake slipped me the mickey."

He looked taken aback at the change of subject. "Beautiful."

"I thought you'd like it. The gown had to go to the cleaners after I got it back from the hospital, but the cloak is beautiful enough to be worn alone."

He dismissed the subject of the cloak impatiently. "Since you won't go to Eric's, I've hired two men to guard you around the clock at your apartment and Sam—"

"Is very sweet. He likes and admires you very much, you know." She tilted her head back and gazed up at the ceiling. "This is a lovely room. Those frescoes on the ceiling are wonderful."

"Are you listening to me, Daisy?"

"Yes, I'm listening." She plopped down in a flurry of white satin on the huge blue velvet, cushioned chesterfield facing the piano. "I'm sure all your arrangements for my safety are very efficient." She smiled lovingly at him. "And it's too bad you wasted all your effort concocting them. I'm not going anywhere, Jason."

"I beg your pardon."

"I'm staying here with you. My suitcases are in the trunk of the limousine. Sam decided to wait to bring them in until you gave him permission."

"Which he isn't going to get."

"Why not? You're not thinking clearly. Your security here is tighter than Eric's house or my apartment could possibly be. Sam can run me back and forth to the theater, and we—"

"It's too dangerous, dammit. Why do you think I wasn't at the theater tonight?"

"Because you're afraid to be close to me," she said gently. "You won't allow me near you because something always happens to people you care about. Don't you see that it's gotten to be a phobia with you?"

"Cynthia's not a phobia, she's a lethal threat."

"One that I'm willing to confront."

"Do you think I don't know that?" he asked hoarsely. "From the moment we met, I realized how generous you are. I knew you'd take any risk for someone you care about."

"So you tried to keep me at a distance." She shook her head. "It's not generosity. I'm being selfish. That homicidal shrew is trying to ruin my life, and I have no intention of letting her get away with it." She paused and then added, "And she's made the man I love go through hell for most of his adult life." She saw him tense and smile faintly. "I'm sorry if you don't want me to say it, but I do love you, Jason."

"Lord knows why. I said you were generous."

"And you love me." She gazed at him pityingly, for he stared at her with a tormented expression twisting his features. "Why won't you tell me, Jason? That chandelier up there isn't going to fall on me just because you say you love me. It's Cynthia, not fate, that's caused all your problems."

"I know that."

"But it's gone on so long you don't believe it." She stood up and reached out and took his hand. "Well, it's time you did. Sit down."

"What?"

She pushed him down onto the easy chair she had just vacated and took a step back. "I've got to convince you how good an idea it is for me to stay here."

"And how do you intend to do that?"

"I have only one weapon in my arsenal that's strong enough to shift the balance." Her hand went to the three jeweled fastenings at the bodice of her cloak. "But it's a weapon we both enjoy using." She slipped the cloak off and let it fall in a silken pool on the carpet.

She ignored the sharp intake of his breath as she sat down on his lap, straddling him, her knees on the cushions on either side of his thighs. "I believe you've neglected my education. I've never made love in a music room."

"You're naked."

"No." She reached back and took off her high-heeled slippers and tossed them on the floor. "*Now* I'm naked." Her eyes twinkled at him. "I told you the cloak was good enough to be worn alone."

"Don't do this to me, Daisy," he said hoarsely. "I can't take it."

"I can." She leaned forward and began unbuttoning his shirt. "All of it. Over and over." She pressed her naked breasts against the hair thatching his chest and felt a shudder rack his body. "As you well know." His heart was beating erratically against her ear, he was hardening against her. She laid her cheek against his shoulder. "Tell me you love me," she whispered.

"Daisy . . ." Her name came out in a strangled rasp.

"All right. Not now." She pressed her lips to the hollow of his throat. "Later."

"Get—off me!"

"Why?" She rubbed against him. The hot tingling between her thighs was becoming an aching emptiness. "You like me here. I can tell."

"Sex."

"Sex is part of love." Her eyes were suddenly shining with tears as she looked up at him. "Don't you see how difficult this is for me? But Charlie told me to go after the brass ring and that's what I have to do. You've always been the brass ring for me. You always will be." She moistened her lips with her tongue. "It's been a long time, Jason. I need you so."

"Do you?" He gazed at her silently for an instant, and his hand reached out and gently touched the bright wing of hair curving against her temple "Daisy . . ."

Then he was fumbling with his clothes, freeing himself. He positioned her, holding her gaze as he slid her slowly onto his arousal.

She cried out as she took him, her teeth sinking into her lower lip.

His arms grabbed her close, taking her breath, holding her sealed to him. The sensation was indescribably full, bold, hot, throbbing. He ground her against him, his chest laboring as he tried to draw breath. "I'm the one in need," he said through gritted teeth. "I've wanted this every time I saw you, every time I looked at you. . . ." His hands curved around her waist, lifting her and bringing her down again with driving force. "Tell me to stop. I'll hurt you. I feel like a wild animal that's—"

"I don't care." Her muscles contracted, squeezing him tighter, and he cried out.

He closed his eyes, panting, shuddering, and then he exploded. Plunging, driving, moving her body to suit himself in a frenzy of passion.

She didn't know how long that frenzy went on, as she was swept along in its wake. She had thought it was too intense to last for long, but somehow it did. Neither of them could get enough of the other. A sensual, erotic haze enveloped her, tinting every breath, coloring every movement in scarlet heat until the climax came to its zenith and released them.

Jason's eyes were still glazed and smoky as his lids lifted to look down at her. "Lord," he whispered.

She nodded, unable to speak for the ripples of aftershock cascading through her body.

He lifted her off him and she slid to her knees on the floor in front of his chair. She was vaguely aware of him putting his clothes in order, but she couldn't move from where she knelt on the floor.

He stood up and snatched the cloak from the floor and put it over her shoulders.

"Thank you," she said automatically.

He looked surprised, and then a small smile tugged at his lips. "I think I should be the one to express thanks." The smile faded. "But it doesn't change anything. You can't stay here."

Daisy wrapped the cloak closer around her. "I thought you'd probably still have arguments, but it certainly broke the ice."

For an instant the grimness vanished from his expression and his lips twitched. "I can't deny it did that."

She moved toward the door, the cloak flowing behind her as she moved. "Where's the kitchen? I'm starved. I hope you don't have any servants in the house to get in my way."

He shook his head. "I have a cleaning service that comes in twice a week."

"Good." She opened the door and glanced back at him. "Come on. I'll make you an omelet."

"In that cloak?"

"Oh, no, I'll take it off before I begin cooking. You must have an apron somewhere. . . ." She glanced over her shoulder. "Coming?"

"You know I am," he said grimly as he started after her. "You deliberately furnish me with that mental picture of you in nothing but an apron, puttering around my kitchen. You're trying to seduce me again, dammit."

"Yep!" She strode ahead of him into the foyer. "I never knew I was capable of seduction, but necessity is a powerful spur. Before this is over I may even become good at it." She shot him a veiled look full of mischief. "Besides, I've never made love in a kitchen either."

"You won't send me away?" she whispered as she cuddled closer to him in the big bed. "It won't do any good. I'll just come back and I'm safer under your protection than chasing after you."

"You pose a strong argument." His lips twisted. "And your persuasiveness is downright irresistible."

"It has to end, Jason. I love you too much to let you be hurt anymore."

He was silent a moment. "Lord, I'm scared for you."

"Don't be. I won't let myself become one of that vixen's victims."

"Easy to say." His voice was uneven. "I'd die for you, Daisy, but I don't think I could stand anything happening to you. It nearly killed me, watching you in that hospital bed when you—"

"Shh, forget about it."

"I can't forget about it." He paused. "This was what I've been afraid of since that first night I saw you. You were everything that was warm and beautiful and shining, and I knew I should turn my back and walk away from you." He buried his face in her hair. "And I couldn't do it. I was so damned hollow and alone. I had to take a little of that shining for myself. Just a little . . ."

"But you gave back too. You gave to me and to Charlie." She kissed his cheek. "Now go to sleep and we'll talk some more in the morning." She paused. "Unless you'd like to make a declaration?"

He drew in a deep breath.

Poor Jason. So afraid to say the words for fear the sky would fall. "Never mind." She yawned as she snuggled closer. "Isn't it exciting? We're actually going to live together. We'll have breakfast and I'll watch you work and you can show me the house. . . ."

"Very exciting," he said gently as he stroked her hair back from her temple.

She was drifting off to sleep when she heard his soft, halting murmur in her ear. It was only one word and not the three she wanted to hear but, nevertheless, the tenderness in his voice soothed and warmed her.

"Shining . . ."

Daisy looked up from her book and said casually, "I have tomorrow night off and I thought I'd try out that space-age kitchen. I invited Peg and Eric for dinner tomorrow night."

"We've already tried out the kitchen. As well as most of the other rooms in the house." Jason didn't look at her as he bent over the keyboard. "And I prefer not to perform in front of guests."

"Lech." Daisy threw her novel aside, stood up, and strolled across the music room toward the piano. "You know what I mean."

"I know exactly what you mean." Jason darted her a smiling glance over his shoulder. "You're trying to save me from my solitude."

"No such thing." She made a face as she sat down beside him on the bench. "Well, maybe. You need to get into the swing of things again."

"You mean behave like a normal human being again.' He shook his head. "Call Eric back and tell him not to come."

"But I think you should—"

His fingers gently touched her lips, silencing her. "No. Not until we can be sure it's safe."

"It's been a week and she hasn't come back. Maybe she'll never come back."

He shook his head. "She's waiting, biding her time."

"You're probably right." She shivered.

He raised a brow. "Where's all that bold optimism you've been bolstering me up with for the last week?"

"It's still there. It just went behind a cloud for a minute. Well, if you won't let me have guests to dinner, there's something else you can give me." She moistened her lips with her tongue and said in a rush, "I've decided I'm tired of being a scarlet woman."

He lifted his gaze to her face. "Indeed?"

She nodded. "Will you marry me, Jason?"

He went still. "Aren't you robbing me of my prerogative?"

"I don't have any choice. You won't reach out and take what you want because you're afraid everything's going to come down around you." She leaned against his shoulder. "So I'm taking the bull by the horns."

"At least you flatter my sexual stamina by the simile."

She ignored the mocking evasion. "Will you make me an honest woman?"

"You were born an honest woman." His lips brushed the tip of her nose. "But it would be my great honor to join with you in marriage."

"I'll try to make it your pleasure too." Daisy looked away from him down at the piano keys. "And I'm glad I won't have to send a retraction to the newspapers."

He stiffened. "Retraction?"

"I sent the papers an announcement of our

engagement. It should be out first in this afternoon's paper."

"Hell and damnation." He muttered a more violent curse beneath his breath and jumped to his feet. "That's a red flag and you know it. Why didn't you just give Cynthia the code for the front gate?"

"If I thought she'd come, I would have taken an ad out in the *Times*." She gazed at him soberly. "We can't live in Shangri-la forever. We have to get on with our lives."

"So you sent out a written invitation to Cynthia to come after you?"

"That's why I told you about the announcement. I thought you'd want to double the precautions."

Jason moved toward the door of the music room. "Nice of you finally to include me in your plans."

"Where are you going?"

"I'm going to call the police and the detective agency and tell them what you've done."

"I wanted to tell you but I knew—" The door slammed behind him, cutting off her sentence.

Daisy stared unhappily at the panels of the door. She had been afraid this would be Jason's reaction. Her description of this last week as living in Shangri-La had been very close to actual fact. It had been a magic time with nights filled with passion and days brimming with work and togetherness. The last thing she had wanted to do was spoil it. Since the first night she had come to Eaglesmount, Jason had carefully kept his fears for her hidden, but she had always been conscious of them lingering like an encroaching darkness in the background.

Well, she had made the only move she could think of to banish the darkness.

Dear heaven, she hoped she hadn't made a mistake.

Ten

Daisy did not see Jason for the rest of the day but found him waiting in the limousine when Sam brought the car around to take her to the theater that evening. His expression was not encouraging. His lips were set and she thought she could sense waves of tension coming from him.

As Sam drove through the gates and started down the winding road to reach the main highway, she said quietly, "You don't have to take me to the theater. I know you'd rather stay here and work."

"What an asinine remark," he said roughly. "What am I supposed to do? Just wait at home for a telephone call to tell me that you've been attacked and kill—" He broke off and reached for the cloak she carried over her arm. "And you don't even have enough sense to put this thing on. You know the hills are cool after the sun goes down." He draped a rust and cream-colored wool cloak over her shoulders with a gentleness that belied the harshness of his tone. "Did you eat supper?"

"I wasn't hungry. I'll grab something after the performance."

"And probably collapse onstage. I'll get you a sandwich after we reach the theater."

"That's not necessary, Jason."

"Yes, it is." He scowled at her. "I may as well watch over you while I still have you to—"

"Don't you dare say it." Her face was suddenly alight with laughter. "Lord, you're a gloomy Gus."

He gazed at her glowing face for a moment before he smiled grudgingly. "Sorry. We all can't shine like you do."

"But you don't have to give me that menacing Othello look either."

"It doesn't phase you anymore. You just tweak my nose and go your own way."

"Because it's good for you to be tweaked occasionally."

His eyes lingered on her face with a warmth that filled her with relief and joy. She hated him to be displeased with her; she hated to have any discord between them.

"You do it more than occasionally." He frowned. "But you deserve a little gloom and doom after the stunt you pulled."

"On the contrary, I deserve praise for my bravery and perseverance . . . and brilliance!" She gave him a half-veiled look and added flippantly, "And if you think I may soon be history, I'd think the least you could do was stop being mad at me."

"I'm not mad at you, I'm merely saying you should have . . ."

She realized he was continuing to speak but lost the thread of his words as she caught a pale glimmer in the rearview mirror.

White and small and gleaming. A car? But they

had not crossed any roads and were still on Eaglesmount property. A car could only have been waiting on one of the shoulders for them to pass.

"Daisy?"

She pulled her gaze from the mirror to Jason's face. "What?"

"Is something wrong?"

It must have been her imagination or an errant glint of fading sunlight on the mirror, for she saw nothing now. "No, I guess I'm just a little nervous."

"It's about time." His hand covered her own. "That's the result I've been hoping to bring about since you moved into Eaglesmount. Not only nervous but as scared as hell. Maybe it will stop you from taking crazy chances."

"Then you've certainly attained your—"

She broke off as the limousine rounded the corner and drove into a sheet of flame!

Sam stomped on the brakes and screeched to a halt. The entire right side of the road had been blocked by an ancient pickup whose cargo of hay and the cab of the vehicle itself was engulfed in flame.

"What the hell!" Jason jumped from the car at the same time as Sam. "Stay here, Daisy I'll see if anyone's still alive." He ran toward the flames.

Dear heaven, what a horror. Daisy got out her side of the limousine and ran toward the pickup. She had to help if she could. It seemed impossible that the driver could have gotten out before—

"*Daisy!*"

Her gaze flew to Jason's face. He was staring at something beyond her shoulder.

She glanced over her shoulder and stopped in the middle of the road, frozen.

A white streak of a sports car barreled down the

road toward her. She caught a glimpse through the windshield of a smiling face framed by lustrous black hair. Cynthia! Terror surged through Daisy, breaking her thrall. She started at a run toward the side of the road.

The sports car was too close!

It was almost upon her!

Then Jason was beside her, snatching her cloak from her shoulders and pushing her to the side with such force she fell to the ground.

What was he going to do?

She knew in the next instant when the car whizzed by her with only a scant inch to spare.

Jason dove after her and, at the same time, hurled her cloak over the windshield of the sports car. The wind instantly plastered the material to the glass.

Daisy heard a shrill scream of panic from inside the car as the blinded woman careened wildly across the highway and then off the road and down the hill.

An explosion rocked the earth and vibrated the tarmac on which Daisy lay. She jumped to her feet and dashed to the edge of the road to see inferno in the valley below. Cynthia's car had rammed into a tree and exploded, and now both the wreckage of the car and the tree itself was in flames.

She heard the sound of the sirens in the distance and saw Sam carefully making his way down the hill toward the wreckage, but she knew it was too late for either of them to help Cynthia Hayes.

"Are you okay?" Jason was beside her, his arm encircling her. "She didn't hurt you?"

"No." She glanced back at the burning pickup

truck. "What about the truck across the road? Was anyone in it?"

"I don't think so. I couldn't see anyone inside. My guess is that she parked the junkheap across the road and then set a radio charge to explode it when she saw us leave the house."

She shivered. "I'm glad no one else is hurt."

"She's dead." Jason's hoarse voice held a note of wonder as he looked down at the flaming car. "It's gone on so long that it's hard to believe it's over." He tore his gaze from the wreckage and looked down at her. "Are you sure the car didn't clip you? You're shaking."

"She didn't hit me." But it had been a terribly close call. She wondered if she was callous not to feel a flicker of regret for the woman who had gone to such a horrible death only a few moments before. Surely every life had value and potential on this earth. Yet she felt nothing but relief that Cynthia Hayes could no longer inflict pain and destruction on those around her. More, she was thankful because Jason would at last be released from darkness. "I'm fine, Jason." She moved closer to him. "We're both going to be fine now."

A long red carpet had been unrolled beneath the elegant steel-gray canopy leading to the rich, dark teakwood doors of the Von Krantz Gallery.

Daisy and Jason arrived an hour before the exhibition was scheduled to open, but already long, gleaming limousines were depositing guests clad in evening wear, and a television truck was parked at the cross street.

Sam let them out before the front entrance of the gallery, but they still had to fight their way through television and newspaper reporters to reach the front door. A gallery assistant unlocked the door, whisked them inside, and then quickly locked the door behind them.

"It's a good thing you called us to be on the alert for you, Mr. Hayes," the chic older woman said. She grimaced. "Everyone wants an advance look at the painting. I'm Mrs. Petersen. Elizabeth Petersen." Her gaze went to Daisy. "The painting lives up to your beauty, Miss Justine. You must be very proud of your father."

"Yes, I am." She smiled. "And it's Mrs. Hayes."

"I'm sorry, I didn't realize that—"

"Nobody does." Daisy took Jason's hand. "We took care of it this afternoon. I confess I wanted to hear how it sounded, but we'd appreciate if you wouldn't tell anyone. We don't want to deflect attention from the exhibition. This is Charlie's night."

"Of course." Mrs. Petersen nodded understandingly. "May I get you a glass of champagne?"

"No," Jason said. "But like the rest of the world, we'd like a preview of 'Daisy.' "

"Certainly, right this way." She led them through the elegantly furnished anteroom. "We're expecting great things from the critics, Mr. Hayes. It's really an extraordinary painting."

"Is it?" Daisy asked eagerly. "You like it?"

Mrs. Petersen raised her brows in surprise. "We'd hardly have accepted the painting if we hadn't believed in it."

"I thought perhaps all the publicity—"

The woman lifted her chin. "We do not enjoy providing a circus for the media at Von Krantz." Her patronizing façade vanished and she added ruefully, "Though it does seem necessary sometimes to encourage the public to embrace a new artist." She had stopped before a silk-draped painting that had been mounted by itself on the far wall. With a flick of a beautifully manicured hand she removed the cloth and took a step back. "Now, if you'll excuse me, I have a million things to do in the next thirty minutes before we open the doors."

"No problem." Jason smiled. "We promise to put the cloth back in place before the media arrive."

Daisy dimly heard the click of Mrs. Petersen's four-inch heels on the polished floor as she walked away, but she couldn't take her gaze from the framed painting.

You've done it, Charlie. You've caught the brass ring at last.

"I didn't expect it to look this impressive," she whispered. "We were too close to it at the cottage, too close to him. She's right, it is extraordinary."

"You should have expected it. It's your portrait. *You're* extraordinary."

She shook her head. "No, this painting isn't about me. It's about love."

"Yes." Jason's arm went around her. "You once said Charlie was good at that."

"He *is* good at that." Her cheeks were flushed, her eyes sparkling with radiance. "Don't you feel it, Jason? Charlie did it! It's all here. It will always be here for you and me and everyone who looks at the painting."

"Yes, I feel it." Jason's voice was husky, his gaze fastened on the painting, and his next words came haltingly. "I . . . love you, Daisy Justine . . . Hayes."

It was the first time he had said the words. She

had known it would take a period of adjustment after all these years before he could accept the love between them without fear for her, and she had tried to be patient as she waited for this final commitment. Now such heady joy surged through her that she had to swallow to ease the sudden tightness of her throat.

Dawn after darkness.

Safety after the storm.

She stepped closer to Jason and lovingly laid her head against his shoulder, but her gaze never left the painting.

Thanks, Charlie.

THE EDITOR'S CORNER

It's a pleasure to return to the Editor's Corner while Susann Brailey is away on maternity leave, the proud mother of her first child—a beautiful, big, healthy daughter. It is truly holiday season here with this wonderful addition to our extended "family," and I'm delighted to share our feelings of blessings with you ... in the form of wonderful books coming your way next month.

First, let me announce that what so many of you have written to me asking for will be in your stockings in just thirty days! Four classic LOVESWEPT romances from the spellbinding pen of Iris Johansen will go on sale in what we are calling the **JOHANSEN JUBILEE** reissues. These much-requested titles take you back to the very beginning of Iris's fabulous writing career with the first four romances she wrote, and they are **STORMY VOWS, TEMPEST AT SEA, THE RELUCTANT LARK,** and **BRONZED HAWK**. In these very first love stories published in the fall and winter of 1983, Iris began the tradition of continuing characters that has come to be commonplace in romance publishing. She is a true innovator, a great talent, and I'm sure you'll want to buy all these signed editions, if not for yourself, then for someone you care about. Could there be a better Christmas present than an introduction to the love stories of Iris Johansen? And look for great news inside each of the JOHANSEN JUBILEE editions about her captivating work coming in February, **THE WIND DANCER**. Bantam, too, has a glorious surprise that we will announce next month.

Give a big shout "hooray" now because Barbara Bowell is back! And back with a romance you've requested—**THE LAST BRADY,** LOVESWEPT

(continued)

#444. Delightful Colleen Brady gets her own romance with an irresistibly virile heartbreaker, Jack Blackledge. He's hard to handle—to put it mildly—and she's utterly inexperienced, so when he needs her to persuade his mother he's involved with a nice girl for a change, the sparks really fly. As always, Barbara Boswell gives you a sweet, charged, absolutely unforgettable love story.

A hurricane hits in the opening pages of Charlotte Hughes's **LOUISIANA LOVIN'**, LOVESWEPT #445, and its force spins Gator Landry and Michelle Thurston into a breathlessly passionate love story. They'd been apart for years, but how could Michelle forget the wild Cajun boy who'd awakened her with sizzling kisses when she was a teenager? And what was she to do with him now, when they were trapped together on Lizard Bayou during the tempest? Fire and frenzy and storm weld them together, but insecurity and pain threaten to tear them apart. A marvelous LOVESWEPT from a very gifted author!

SWEET MISCHIEF, LOVESWEPT #446, by Doris Parmett is a sheer delight. Full of fun, fast-paced, and taut with sexual tension, **SWEET MISCHIEF** tells the love story of sassy Katie Reynolds and irresistible Bill Logan. Bill is disillusioned about the institution of marriage and comes home to his childhood friend Katie with an outrageous proposition. . . . But Katie has loved him long enough and hard enough to dare anything, break any rules to get him for keeps. Ecstasy and deep emotion throw Bill for a loop . . . and Katie is swinging the lasso. **SWEET MISCHIEF** makes for grand reading, indeed. A real keeper.

Bewitching is the first word that comes to mind to
(continued)

describe Linda Cajio's LOVESWEPT #447, **NIGHTS IN WHITE SATIN**. When Jill Daneforth arrives in England determined to get revenge for the theft of her mother's legacy, she is totally unprepared for Rick Kitteridge, an aristocrat and a devil of temptation. He pursues her with fierce passion—but an underlying fear that she can never be wholly his, never share more than his wild and wonderful embraces. How this tempestuous pair reconciles their differences provides some of the most exciting reading ever!

Witty and wonderful, **SQUEEZE PLAY,** LOVESWEPT #448, from beloved Lori Copeland provides chuckles and warmth galore. As spontaneous as she is beautiful, Carly Winters has to struggle to manage her attraction to Dex Mathews, the brilliant and gorgeous ex-fiance who has returned to town to plague her in every way . . . including competing in the company softball game. They'd broken up before because of her insecurity over their differences in everything except passion. Now he's back kissing her until she melts, vowing he loves her as she is . . . and giving you unbeatable romance reading.

Sweeping you into a whirlwind of sensual romance, **LORD OF LIGHTNING,** LOVESWEPT #449, is from the extraordinary writer, Suzanne Forster. Lise Anderson takes one look at Stephen Gage and knows she has encountered the flesh-and-blood embodiment of her fantasy lover. As attracted to her as she is to him, Stephen somehow knows that Lise yearns to surrender to thrilling seduction, to abandon all restraint. And he knows, too, that he is just the man to make her dreams come true. But her fears collide with his . . . even as they show

(continued)

each other the way to heaven . . . and only a powerful love can overcome the schism between this fiercely independent schoolteacher and mysterious geologist. **LORD OF LIGHTNING**—as thrilling a romance as you'll ever hope to read.

Six great romances next month . . . four great Iris Johansen classics—LOVESWEPT hopes to make your holiday very special and very specially romantic.

With every good wish for a holiday filled with the best things in life—the love of family and friends.

Sincerely,

Carolyn Nichols

Carolyn Nichols,
Publisher,
LOVESWEPT
Bantam Books
666 Fifth Avenue
New York, NY 10103

P.S. GIVE YOURSELF A SPECIAL PRESENT: CALL OUR LOVESWEPT LINE 1-900-896-2505 TO HEAR EXCITING NEWS FROM ONE OF YOUR FAVORITE AUTHORS AND TO ENTER OUR SWEEPSTAKES TO WIN A FABULOUS TRIP FOR TWO TO PARIS!

FOREVER LOVESWEPT

SPECIAL KEEPSAKE EDITION OFFER

$12⁹⁵

VALUE

Here's your chance to receive a special hardcover Loveswept "Keepsake Edition" to keep close to your heart forever. Collect hearts (shown on next page) found in the back of Loveswepts #426-#449 (on sale from September 1990 through December 1990). Once you have collected a total of 15 hearts, fill out the coupon and selection form on the next page (no photocopies or hand drawn facsimiles will be accepted) and mail to: Loveswept Keepsake, P.O. Box 9014, Bohemia, NY 11716.

FOREVER LOVESWEPT
SPECIAL KEEPSAKE EDITION OFFER
SELECTION FORM

Choose from these special Loveswepts by your
favorite authors. Please write a 1 next to your first
choice, a 2 next to your second choice. Loveswept
will honor your preference as inventory allows.

_____BAD FOR EACH OTHER   Billie Green

_____NOTORIOUS   Iris Johansen

_____WILD CHILD   Suzanne Forster

_____A WHOLE NEW LIGHT   Sandra Brown

_____HOT TOUCH   Deborah Smith

_____ONCE UPON A TIME...GOLDEN
     THREADS   Kay Hooper

Attached are 15 hearts and the selection form which
indicates my choices for my special hardcover Loveswept
"Keepsake Edition." Please mail my book to:

NAME:_____

ADDRESS:_____

CITY/STATE:_____ZIP:_____

Offer open only to residents of the United States, Puerto Rico and
Canada. Void where prohibited, taxed, or restricted. Allow 6 - 8
weeks after receipt of coupons for delivery. Offer expires
January 15, 1991. You will receive your first choice as inventory
allows; if that book is no longer available, you'll receive your
second choice, etc.